SEXY

SPOOKY

SEASON

LOVE FEY

Dedication

To all the sexy, spooky bitches out there.

To all the book girlies who love a masked MMC.

To all the grown women who would swoon at being called *baby girl* by a big dude in a haunted house.

This one is for you!

(And for me…it's for me, too.)

Content Warning

Sexy Spooky Season is an erotic romance. All of the sex scenes are with the door thrown happily wide open. There are detailed descriptions of all the acts involved. Consider this your fair warning. However, this story is NOT a dark romance in anyway. While there's nothing wrong with dark romances, my goal in writing this story was to take the masked male main character trope, keep the sexiness, mystery, and intensity, but eliminate the darker content. I am thrilled with the outcome.

Below is a more thorough list of what you will encounter between the pages of this novella. Keep in mind that these are the main content warnings and may not cover smaller warnings that are specific from reader-to-reader. Take care, dear reader.

Explicit Language
Graphic Sexual Content
Masturbation (MMC)
Fellatio
Cunnilingus
Sex in Public Places
Handcuff Usage (during foreplay)
Self-Harm/Attempted Suicide (past, discussed)

If these are okay with you, please proceed.

Happy reading!

1

All Horrors' Eve

"Through the eyeholes of his mask, Lark saw her, and everything crystalized in that beautiful and startling moment. She was stunning, with black hair that feathered like raven's wings and brushed her pale shoulders. Those strands of ebony hair skimmed against her neck, and that was how he noticed the scar that stretched from one side of her neck to the other, just above her collarbone. His entire body tensed at the sight of the pale pink line—so pretty, so mysterious. There was a story there that he yearned to know.

How'd she get it? *When* did she get it? The fact she wasn't trying to hide it with a necklace or little scarf or even with makeup meant she wasn't ashamed of it.

In his opinion, she shouldn't be ashamed of it. Her scar was a part of her, and he desired to get to know her *and* her scar. He fisted his hands at his sides to dispel the need to trail the tips of his fingertips over that scar, to feel the silkiness of the healed flesh and the hard line where her skin had sealed back together. His needs were so intense that he clenched his jaw as he imagined kissing and licking it.

His gaze trailed down the rest of her. She wore a black tank top, jean shorts, and black sneakers. Her legs were long and her thighs gorgeous as she walked and they skimmed together. Beneath his pumpkin mask, he ran his teeth over his bottom lip. The urge to part those thighs and settle his head between them, feel them clench around his skull was fierce. He'd never had such a whiplash surge of lust before, but holy shit he wanted her.

She was with a group of friends, though—two men and three women. Neither of the guys were close, so he hoped that meant she wasn't with either of them. She was next to a woman with unnatural mahogany hair, though. Were they together? They were laughing. They were whispering. Then the woman with mahogany hair peered to the side and winked.

Lark followed her line of sight to where Cal in a skull mask stood. Okay. So Mahogany Hair was into men. At least men in skull masks who worked at Halloween theme parks like All Horrors' Eve. So hopefully that meant his scarred angel was single.

As they walked closer, he stepped out of the shadows.

She looked right at him.

The force of her stare halted him. He was a trained scare actor. Normal people weren't supposed to make

2

him freeze like a startled idiot, but she'd stunned him.

A small smile played on her lips.

She wasn't dressed like the other women who were there, hoping to get fucked by a masked man for a story to post to social media. No, his scarred angel was dressed because of the humid Florida night. Nor did she seem to be there to get railed by a masked man. Not like her friend who wore what equated to a black bra and was throwing "I want you to fuck me hard" looks at his friend who would surely take her up on that offer.

His scarred angel shifted her gaze away.

Beside her, Mahogany Hair said something. Then she left his angel's side, heading toward Cal, who stepped closer, towering and menacing and aware that both were turning Mahogany Hair on. Everyone who was within eyesight was aware of it.

His angel shook her head and continued on with her friends. Lark followed several paces behind, staking his claim. His other scare actor friends noticed. They all had a code. If one of them clearly picked someone for the night, they were off limits. The others targeted her friends to taunt and tease, but they left his angel alone. Did she notice? Did she sense him behind her?

The night was hot. Howls and screeches, screams and hideous laughter filled the humid air. Sweat dotted Lark's forehead and upper lip beneath his pumpkin mask. A bead of sweat slithered a path down his spine. Although he was shirtless with just a distressed leather vest on, the heat was stifling.

His angel was hot, too. She lifted her black tank, twisted the cotton around her finger, and tucked it into the middle of her bra.

The sight of her back and waist and the beginning shape of her hips glistening with a sheen of sweat thickened his cock in his black cargo pants.

Desire pumped through his veins. He wanted nothing more than to back her against a building and lick the sweat from her stomach and from between her breasts and thighs. He craved her salt, her water, her skin—everything.

She glanced over her shoulder.

Yeah, I'm here, angel.

She didn't stop walking.

He didn't stop following.

But the longer he trailed after her, the harder he became. He wasn't innocent compared to his friends. It wasn't like he didn't choose a pretty little thing on occasion, lure her into the darkness, and have a little fun. He did that from time to time when one caught his eye and was willing, but he didn't do it nearly as often as his friends, who made a selection every night. Sometimes two or three times in one night. Even several of them at once. He'd heard the stories. He'd stumbled across Cal with a man and two women. Cal was eating out one woman, thrusting his cock into the other, while the man pumped into him from behind. Lark had never seen anything like it. He hustled out of there as quickly as he could and jerked off alone. The way he was now, because of his scarred angel's sweaty, swaying body, he would need a release fast.

When she and her friends stepped into the line for the Ferris wheel, he slunk off down a random alley. His cock was a bulge in his pants, straining against the zipper. If he didn't find privacy soon, the zipper's track would be imprinted on the head of his penis. His pace quickened. He grabbed his cock and squeezed just as he erupted out of the alley.

Moans had him spinning to the right.

Cal, still wearing his skull mask, leaned against the back of the haunted house with his pants open and his cock out. Mahogany Hair was on her knees in front of him, with her mouth around Cal's cock. His hands gripped her head. His fingers tangled with that mahogany hair as he dragged her head back and forth.

Cal angled his head toward Lark and nodded his head in silent acknowledgment. While looking at him, Cal forced Mahogany Hair to take his cock deeper into her throat. Lark stood there a moment, rooted in place while palming his cock and watching the woman taking Cal without resistance but with an apparent eagerness that had pre-cum gushing from Lark's dick.

He staggered down the alley behind the buildings to the wooden gate that circled the park. In the corner, he ripped off his leather glove, shoved it into his pocket, and whipped out his cock. He worked his fist up and down his length to the vision of his angel's body and the sounds of Mahogany Hair sucking Cal off. His friend's groans and the slurping of Mahogany Hair's mouth encouraged him. He could almost imagine that his hand was his angel's mouth around his dick and those slurping sounds were coming from her. With his eyelids squeezed shut, it was the truth.

Behind him, Cal was getting close to climaxing.

The sucking became more frenzied.

Lark pumped his hand faster.

Cal groaned long and deep as he came in

5

Mahogany Hair's mouth.

A lewd popping sound of her mouth pulling off Cal's cock met Lark's ears.

He focused on the sensation of his fist tightening around his dick. His angel's waist, her hips encased in jeans, her bare thighs, the sleek plain of her back—he replayed all of that in his mind. She was his little mystery...his raging lust. He wished she were there, replacing his hand.

"Hey, man." Cal's voice cut through Lark's thoughts. "If you need some help, Trina can finish you off."

So Mahogany Hair's name is Trina.

"I'd be happy to," a woman's voice said.

He was sure she would be happy to, especially after the way she finished off Cal, but Lark didn't want her, so he shook his head.

"Alright," Cal said. "Let's give him some privacy."

Lark listened to them leave.

As soon as he was alone, he pumped his hand more aggressively. *Fuck*. A snapshot of her scar blazed through his thoughts and burned his mind with passion unlike any he'd ever felt before. *Fuck, fuck, fuck*. He was close. His grip tightened. He dragged his hand faster and faster over his cock. Thinking of her scar, imagining kissing it and licking it and his cum slicking it, he came. He came so hard that he couldn't stop a grunt from breaking out of his weak vocal cords. His cum splashed onto the wood fence in front of him.

Panting, heart racing, he stuffed his semi-hard cock back into his pants. Then he braced the hand that had been around his cock on the fence and used his gloved hand to massage his throat. His vocal cords throbbed. Grimacing, he probed his throat. His vocal cords would probably hurt for the next two days because of that.

Worth it.

Still massaging his throat, he turned. And froze. His scarred angel was there, staring with wide eyes.

"I...I'm sorry," she said. "I was looking for my friend. I thought maybe she was with you, but..." She studied the fence behind him. "...you're alone."

He glanced back at his cum dripping down the front of the fence. Meeting her eyes, he nodded. *I was alone, but now I'm with you.*

"I'll go now. Sorry."

When she went to leave, he lowered his hand from his neck and held it out.

She stilled. Her gaze drifted to the cum-streamed fence again. "Um. Do you usually jerk off in alleys while the park is open?"

He lifted a shoulder—sometimes he did jerk off in alleys while the park was open—and he advanced to see if she'd back away.

She didn't. "What...if I may ask...inspired that?"

He advanced another step. Staring through the eyeholes of his mask, he lifted a hand and pointed a finger at her.

"Me?"

He nodded.

"What about me?"

Everything, angel. Everything. He raised a hand to indicate her entire being.

She peered down. "I guess lifting up my shirt like that is quite dramatic and can be seen as 'asking for it.'"

Oh, fuck. No, angel, that's not what I meant. Fuck. He vigorously shook his head and stretched out his hand. She didn't back away or swat at his hand, so he was able to trace her scar with his gloved finger. When he reached the end of it, he was awarded with seeing her shiver.

"My scar?" Her voice was a breath. "Did you get off to my scar?"

He knocked his head to the side in a gesture he meant as "maybe" even while he thought, *definitely*.

She swallowed. "Open thyroid surgery. Two years ago. I had thyroid tumors. My doctors were worried about them, but they were benign. Left behind an ugly scar, though."

He shook his head slowly.

"You don't think it's hideous?"

More head shakes.

"Most people do."

Most people are assholes. He continued to trace her scar.

"Well, I guess you wouldn't think it's hideous if you jerked off while thinking about it. Do you have a scar kink?"

He lifted a shoulder. *Possibly*. But so far, her scar was the only one that had turned him on.

A smile like the one she gave him before lifted her lips. "Do you speak or is this a part of the role you're playing? You're the silent stalker?"

He tilted his head. *No, I don't speak, angel, but that doesn't have to get in our way. Does it?* He would get on his knees to show her that he hoped it wouldn't be a problem. He didn't need a voice to show her how she made him feel. He certainly didn't need a voice to make her feel good.

"Sutton!"

She flinched back. "I have to go."

Before he could do a thing, she was gone, returning to her friends.

Sutton.

Such a pretty and interesting name for his angel.

He inhaled. On the exhale, he made an "s" sound like a hissing snake. The "ugh" for the "u" was easy. Like a breath. Focusing all his attention on his tongue, he formed the "t" and "n" sounds. His attempt was clunky. He attempted it again. "Sssu...tn." Another long inhale. "Sssu...ton." That was probably the best he'd manage without therapy.

He'd lost his ability to speak following a car accident when he was eighteen—vocal cord paralysis. Every once in a while, he could produce a voice, but his pitch was limited to what barely qualified as a whisper. He didn't have trouble breathing, and he only had difficulties swallowing when he accidentally strained his vocal cords, like what he'd probably just done.

Years ago, he attended speech therapy, but he'd stopped going when he became frustrated that his pitch wouldn't ever rise above a whisper. And the pain following the appointments sucked.

He gazed off toward where Sutton had scurried away to rejoin her friends. Maybe he'd go back to therapy. The pain would be worth it if he could say her name the way her name was meant to be said.

2

Mr. Horny Pumpkin Mask

Sutton! Do I have to send out a search party?"

Sutton laughed as she stepped out of the alley. "No, I'm right here."

Trina glanced behind Sutton. "Did you just come from the alley?"

"Yeah."

"Were you alone?"

Perhaps best to lie and keep her encounter with the man in the pumpkin mask to herself. "Yeah."

Trina grinned. "Well, I wasn't when I was back there."

Sutton stiffened. "Oh, who were you with?"

"The tattooed guy with a skull mask."

Sutton's shoulders relaxed.

"I went down on him back there. And then this

10

horny guy in a sexy but creepy pumpkin mask appeared and started to stroke himself, so Skull Mask fucked me behind the games, up against the dart booth. It was the hottest thing ever. All of it. Even Mr. Horny Pumpkin Mask wanking off."

Trina was the type to look for thrills fucking strangers, especially of the masked variety. If it wasn't scare actors at Halloween theme parks, carnivals, or fairs, then it was sexy guests who came to their adult haunted house every spooky season. In fact, Sutton and Trina were at All Horrors' Eve to have fun before the grand opening of Haunted House of Raunch tomorrow.

They rejoined their friends in line for cotton candy.

"What should we do next?" Donna asked as she lifted her brown hair from her neck and fanned her sweaty, olive-toned skin.

"The zero-gravity ride," Mavis said while taking her mountain of cotton candy from the vendor.

Sutton peered at the ride in the shape of a UFO as it spun so quickly it became a blur of colors. Her throat tightened. She'd gone on that ride when she was little and hated it; she didn't want to step a foot into that contraption. "We should go to the haunted house."

"Zero gravity ride first and then the haunted house," Ralph said while passing everyone their cotton candy.

Sutton accepted hers, tore off a clump of spun sugar, and let the wispy bits of sugar dissolve on her tongue. Walking through the park, she spied on the scare actors doing their thing and how the girls giggled and flirted, either pretending not to be scared or overdoing their fear.

She lowered her gaze to the cotton candy in her hand and extracted another pinch of pink fluff. When she raised her head, she spotted the man in the creepily sexy pumpkin mask. He sat on a wooden barrel at the entrance of an alley, with his back against a building.

Trina nudged Sutton with an elbow. "That's him. Mr. Horny Pumpkin Mask."

Sutton checked him out in a way she'd been too shocked to do when she walked in on him finishing himself off. He wore black cargo pants, combat boots, biker gloves, and a distressed leather vest that showed off his bare chest and abs. She'd never seen such a sculpted body in person. He clearly crafted that body from discipline and dedication...discipline and dedication that was sexy as hell.

Even with that mask on, he oozed sex appeal, and she felt it. She felt it when he tilted his head to the side, looking right at her, appraising her. The memory of his gloved finger skimming over her scar made her shiver.

His legs were spread, and he held a bat between them. He hadn't had a bat before. Where'd he get it? The answer to that didn't matter when he rolled his body, and his gloved fingers opened and closed slowly around the handle of the bat. It was a purely sexual move that struck her right to the core.

Trina leaned into Sutton. "I think I'm pregnant."

"I think the bat is pregnant," Sutton whispered. "And you very well could be considering you banged Skull Mask."

"Worth having to take the morning after pill."

Sutton resisted mentioning STI's, because looking at Mr. Horny Pumpkin Mask, she felt the same reckless urges building inside her.

"Mm. He's fine as hell. That pumpkin mask just makes him sexier."

Sutton agreed. She couldn't look away as their group ambled closer. Had anyone who visited Haunted House of Raunch ever been turned on by one of them as she was by this half-naked, masked man? He was breathing deeply, drawing her gaze to his abs again. The way his body moved, it spoke of lust and urges. Was this just a part of his script: act like you're ravenous for the people walking past?

Or was he aroused again?

His other hand rubbed down his abs to his legs, where he grabbed his dick and pulled up on his crotch.

"And I'm wet," Trina whispered.

As they walked past, he shoved to his feet, revealing the deepest sex-line cuts in his lower abdomen. He lifted his bat and braced it across his shoulders. The action put his glorious, glistening chest on full display.

Holy shit. Her cheeks blazed with heat.

His feasting stare gave her chills. After a moment, she couldn't stop herself from peeking over her shoulder, but he was gone.

"Zero-gravity time," Mavis cheered.

Dread washed over Sutton. "I'm going to pass."

"Oh, come on." Mavis held Sutton's hand with her pale hands and tugged. "Come with us."

Sutton shook her head. "Not happening."

"It's okay," Trina said. "Sutton will wait for us, and then we'll all go to the haunted house." She ushered their friends off and glanced back at Sutton.

"Thank you," Sutton mouthed.

Trina nodded.

While her friends got into the line for the zero-gravity ride, she sat on a bench and watched them make their way up the steps and disappear into the UFO. The door closed them inside. The UFO began to spin, and she shifted away. She couldn't even watch the damn ride.

A plastic machete flashed in front of her face, and she looked up at a scare actor with fake blood smeared across his chest. He set the tip of the fake blade beneath her chin. She didn't so much as flinch. But her eyes did widen when a bat appeared, putting a barrier between her and the scare actor. Her gaze ticked over to the man in the pumpkin mask.

At the same time, the scare actor turned. The second he saw who was there, he lifted a hand and backed away. "Sorry, man. She's all yours."

Sutton blinked.

The man in the pumpkin mask squatted in front of her.

"I'm yours?" she asked, arching a brow.

He raised a shoulder in a slight shrug.

"Am I supposed to be your victim? Because I'm the furthest thing from a victim. And if you think you're scaring me, you couldn't be more wrong."

The sound of his breathing—slow, deep inhales and exhales—lured her in.

"I don't scare easily. Or at all." She leaned forward. "A strange man in a creepy mask does nothing to me but turn me on." She rose to her feet.

He eyed her crotch before he stood, too.

She stilled when his gloved hand curled around her waist. His hand clenched her side briefly before relaxing, but he didn't take his hand away. This was nothing like the gentle brush of his gloved finger over her scar. This was intentional…sexual.

"Is this a part of your schtick? Pick a pretty girl and play with her? See if she'll play back? Do you pick a new girl every night? A few a night if you're ambitious?"

He exhaled noisily, hinting at veiled anger. Then his hand on her waist lifted to embrace the side of her face. His thumb stroked her cheek. The gentleness he exhibited was startling, and the feel of the leather grazing her skin gave her a chill.

Peering into her eyes, he shook his head.

"You don't pick a new girl to toy with every night?"

Another head shake.

"Is this because of my scar?"

He angled his head slowly.

The action was hot, but a head tilt wasn't an answer.

"Turning you on is one benefit of having this scar."

He removed his glove and traced her scar again. His thumb paused in the middle of her throat as she swallowed.

"The other benefit is that I can play a joker who'd had her throat slit without any makeup effects."

Through the eyeholes, his lashes lowered slowly as he squinted.

"Yeah, I'm a scare actor, too. I work at an adult haunted house. I'm the sexy, chaotic joker. Lock up your spouses because none are safe with me."

He gripped her waist with both hands now and tugged her closer, but she flattened a hand to his chest. His skin was hot beneath her palm and his chest so rock-solid that it stole her breath.

"You're breaking a lot of rules right now," she whispered.

He nodded; he seemed to only speak with nods and shrugs. Even so, he was magnetic. She couldn't deny that he was arousing her with the way he grasped her waist or how he stared at her through those holes in his mask.

Wondering if he could feel how her body buzzed with desire, she slipped out of his grasp and walked away.

3

Funhouse of Mirrors

*L*ark watched her leave, although every part of him revved with the need to chase after her and beg her to stay with his eyes, with his hands, with whatever whisper he could get out of his vocal cords.

She headed for the funhouse of mirrors. Just before she stepped inside, she glanced over her shoulder. The look she gave him told him to follow.

He sprang forward to answer that voiceless call.

Inside the funhouse, the atmosphere was dark with the occasional flash of strobe lights. Strange music seeped from the speakers. His own reflection filled the mirrors around him. He'd never entered the funhouse before. Couldn't say he liked it very much, but he yearned to be near Sutton, and if that look wasn't a

17

clear invitation, then…

He caught a glimpse of her in the mirrors before she disappeared. *Where are you going, beautiful?* He slipped past a mirror to only see more mirrors that distorted his reflection into alien shapes. Because he'd never been through the funhouse, he had no idea which way to go, but Sutton apparently knew how to navigate the maze of mirrors because no matter where he went, she wasn't there.

"Marco!"

He couldn't call out Polo.

Jaw clenched, he rounded another corner. Still no sight of her.

"Are you coming for me?"

Yeah, angel, I'm coming.

"You came for me earlier, but now I want you to come for me again."

He gripped the edge of a mirror. *Holy fuck. Did she really just say that?* His dick twitched in his pants as his entire body tensed with desire. He inched around the mirror. With each step, his penis thickened at the anticipation of finding her. The possibilities of what could happen once he found her filled his mind with erotic visions that encouraged him to full, excruciating erection.

"Do you think you can find me?" Her voice echoed.

Oh, I'll find you. He rounded a mirror and halted.

Her gorgeous reflection filled the mirrors surrounding him. He rotated in a circle. Was one of them real? He held out a hand. The tips of his fingers met with cold glass. He followed the circumference of the space, trailing his fingers over her reflection, hoping that one of them would be the flesh of her stomach and not cool, smooth glass.

Suddenly, she darted away, and her reflection disappeared.

Damn it. You need to stay still, angel.

A teasing whistle bounced off the walls.

Now who is toying with whom?

He followed her whistle through the maze until the sound stopped. His feet halted with it. Searching, he scanned the mirrors. No reflection but his own. Becoming frustrated with this game, he stormed around the next corner and the next. He was stomping toward a gap between two mirrors when her reflection appeared.

"Which reflection is real?"

He rotated, sure that she was behind him.

"Which one am I?"

Now she sounded as though she was at his back again, so he spun around.

"Do you think you're close?"

He held perfectly still and only shifted his gaze from side to side, trying to figure out which reflection real.

All the reflections stepped forward.

He didn't move.

The reflections lowered to their knees.

He sucked in a breath.

Hands clutched his hips.

He peered down at Sutton in front of him.

Staring up at him, she lowered the zipper to his pants. She broke eye contact to reach in and draw his cock out. Her fingers curled around him, and her fingers were so much better than his own.

Fuck.

She met his eye again, with his cock inches from her mouth. "Come for me again." Her breath blasted the head of his penis.

He seethed between his teeth from the heat of her breath. Then her lips parted, and she leaned forward, taking his cock into her mouth. He braced a hand on the mirror behind her as her tongue swirled around him.

Beneath his mask, his eyelids fluttered. She danced that tongue of hers around his girth as if tasting him was an experience like trying a decadent dessert for the first time. Fuck, she was treating his cock like a decadent dessert.

"Mm." And she was moaning.

She inched back only to take him deeper and twirl that sleek, hot tongue. Several times she did that, withdrawing and returning and using her tongue to savor his cock. When his hand fisted against the mirror, she finally took him to the back of her throat. The groan that rattled his vocal cords had him gripping his neck. He pressed his fingers to either side of his esophagus to try to halt any other sounds of pleasure that could hurt him.

But the way she was sucking on him, it'd be impossible not to make a sound.

She drew him in and out. When the pace of her bobbing head quickened, he shoved his knuckles into the mirror. Any harder and he imagined the glass shattering. Even then, he hoped she wouldn't stop.

Her throat accepted him. The tightness had him trying to speak, to express the incredible pleasure.

"Fu—"

That was all he could get out. On a breath, over and over, just the first half of *fuck* could make it past his lips. His vocal cords didn't want to cooperate to make the harsh click of the second half of the word. Only someone who once had been able to speak knew how much it sucked not being able to say "fuck" when a woman's mouth was doing such amazing things to your cock.

She moaned with his cock deep.

The vibrations were too damn good.

His body tensed, and he couldn't stop his hips from jutting forward. He clamped his hand around his neck as he came and purged his cum down the tight confines of her throat. She swallowed, and that single act as she drank his cum encouraged more cum to pump free.

Jesus, it felt amazing to be in her mouth.

She eased back and licked her lips.

Still holding his neck, he tucked his cock away.

She stood. "Are you okay?"

He nodded.

"You keep holding your throat. You were doing that before."

The fingers of his right hand fluttered with the urge to sign, but she wouldn't understand what he'd say anyway. And he didn't want to freak her out. He'd seen that happen. How would she react upon finding out he could only ever truly speak through American Sign Language? Would she flee like the others?

He didn't want to hear the polite words of rejection coming from her lips before she beat a hasty exit, so he lowered his hand. Rather than find some way to answer, he placed his hand on her hip and backed her into the mirror. His craving was fierce. He attacked the button on her jeans, popping it open, and wrenched down her zipper. But her hands halted his when he attempted to tug those little shorts down.

She swiped his fingers away and undid all his work. "If you want to feast, you're going to have to hunt for your dinner."

I just hunted you down so you could eat. Now, I have to hunt you down again so I can eat? That's not fair, sweetheart.

She slipped away. "Close your eyes."

He could do nothing else but obey.

"And count to ten. Then come find me."

He closed his eyes.

His ears picked up the sound of her darting off.

One...

4

Baby Girl

utton's body hummed with primal needs and excitement as she snaked through the rest of the funhouse of mirrors. She'd never done anything like that before. At least, not with a stranger whose face she'd never seen, whose name she didn't know, whose voice she'd never heard. Not strangers, no, but she wasn't immune to the power of a good mask and a good railing.

Her parents had owned a Halloween shop that had been open year-round. She'd worked there from the age of fourteen to twenty-two. Her very first boyfriend had taken her virginity on the floor of the Halloween shop, down Aisle 6 where the men's costumes were. He'd worn the Ghostface mask the entire time. In fact, she figured the Ghostface mask had tempted her into having sex with him. He'd been chasing her around the shop after they'd closed, and when he'd caught her, she'd wanted to be truly and thoroughly taken.

She'd dated and banged other employees who'd worked at the Halloween shop. Each time, they'd been in a costume that'd made the whole thing delicious and sinful. Later, when she created Haunted House of Raunch, she tended to cave every now and then and have some sweaty fun with a fellow scare actor after a particularly exciting night. She just never went for the guests. Not like Trina who enjoyed the thrill of having sex with someone she didn't know.

Here Sutton was, though, moments after going down on a scare actor inside a funhouse, while the park was open. Anyone could've seen her with a strange man's cock in her mouth. A teenager could've come across them. And yet, the possibility of getting caught had only thrilled her more.

She wasn't done, either. Now, she was desperate for him to catch her and eat her as she knew he was ravenous to do, but where did she want it to happen? She could get onto the Ferris wheel and have him join her in the car, but other people would be nearby, so she'd have to be quiet…she couldn't guarantee that she'd be silent.

Her gaze landed on the haunted house across the way. No one was in line, and she didn't see her friends anywhere. Inside the haunted house, it'd be dark with plenty of hiding places. It would be perfect. She made her way to the other side of the paved road. At the entrance, she peered back and saw her Mr. Horny Pumpkin Mask emerge from the funhouse. She smiled before parting the black curtain and slipping inside the haunted house.

The first section was a graveyard. A man in a skull mask snuck up on her. He was tall and bore down on her in an attempt to intimidate her with his size and scare her with his mask and the way he eyed her. She wondered if this was the man Trina had had a good time with earlier.

She gave him a polite smile before sidestepping him.

When she edged around him, though, she found a whole gang of men in skull masks slithering out of the shadows. They surrounded her on all sides so she couldn't move. Their biceps were large. Some wore skin-tight black shirts, a few had on tanks that hugged their muscular shoulders, and others were shirtless. Several were tattooed. Ink marred their chests and arms. A few were inkless but no less intriguing. Being trapped by them with nowhere to go, Sutton couldn't stop her arousal from building. Nor could she help but visualize all of them taking care of her in worshipping ways. She didn't know if this was usual in the haunted house, if they came out to tease everyone who ventured inside, but it felt dangerous and sexy all at once.

One growled under his breath. And then another.

She shivered.

"I think you made a wrong turn, baby girl."

Holy shit.

They didn't even have the scare actors say *baby girl* in Haunted House of Raunch. Big mistake. If book girlies knew masked men were growling and calling them baby girl in their haunted house, they'd always have a line. They'd never go broke.

Trina would love this.

"We can show you the way, sweetheart."

"Come with us."

A wet heat dripped from her pussy.

The man in front of her who had called her baby girl peered over her head. Then he backed away and disappeared into the shadows. One by one, they all vanished. But someone was still there. Behind her. Creeping. Spying.

She rotated.

The man in the pumpkin mask stood several feet away.

She stepped back.

He crept closer.

She watched him as she created more distance between them. Why did the skull masks leave like that after seeing the man with the pumpkin mask? Was his presence that strong? Did he ooze "she's mine" vibes?

The way he was so focused on her as he inched nearer, she believed it. They all were aware that she was his, because she *was* his. At least in this moment.

She backed through the wispy gauze that divided the next section of the haunted house. Fake corn sprouted from both sides of the path. As she made her way down, hands like *Jeepers Creepers* attempted to snatch her. She dodged the hands and hurried to the next section. Scare actors jumped out left and right. She didn't react to their attempts to frighten her.

Down a tight hall between attractions, Sutton found herself alone. No scare actors lurked there. She spotted a strip of black fabric that covered a hiding spot where a scare actor could be lurking. A peek behind the fabric showed that no one was behind it, so she snuck into the space. Using her finger, she peered out. Her body jittered with excitement.

Pumpkin Mask stepped into the hallway and paused.

She held perfectly still and captured her breath in her lungs.

He stood there as if listening for her, trying to detect where she was. She didn't dare move. After a moment, he stepped through the next curtain.

She slipped out of her hiding place. Now she was the one stalking him.

The next attraction of the haunted house was meant to delay the guests to give the scare actors a chance to prepare. The room was decked out with gore. Red paint dripped down the walls to look like blood sprays. Jars on tables were full of foods pickled to resemble organs.

Pumpkin Mask scanned the room.

On tiptoe, she snuck up behind him. "Boo."

He spun around.

"Did you work up an appetite?"

His hands cupped her hips, and he backed her against the fake-blood splattered wall.

"I guess you did," she whispered.

He skimmed his fingers up the inside of her thighs.

Staring into the eyeholes of his mask, unable to make out the color of his irises, she opened her legs.

His fingers stroked her through her jeans.

The friction had her moaning.

He leaned into her and settled his face beside her neck. She couldn't feel his breath on her skin, because he still wore the mask, but she could feel his left hand squeezing her waist and, of course, the fingers of his right hand caressing her between her legs. Those fingers played like he wanted her to come on her panties, and she would if he didn't stop.

She wrapped her hand around his wrist. "Wait."

He shook his head.

"Yes." She clasped his hand. "Over here." She led him back to the hall and into the hiding place. The space was cramped, confining his shoulders. He shifted sideways, and she slid into the gap between him and the wall. They stood so close that she could feel his erection between her legs. She laid her hands on his shoulders and pushed. "On your knees."

He dropped on command.

Seeing that eagerness had her jittering. "Take off my shorts."

He popped the button with a snap, wrenched down the zipper, and tugged her jeans past her thighs. They tumbled around her ankles, and her cell phone, that had been in her back pocket, thumped onto the floor.

She stepped out of her shorts, and he caught her hips. Then he buried his face between the apex of her thighs. The sound of him inhaling stole her breath. His tongue probed her clit through the cotton of her panties, and her entire body jolted from the contact, and it wasn't even direct contact. He continued to tease her like that, though, wetting the cotton with his tongue. The way the wet cotton rubbed against her clit beneath his tongue made her quiver. Once again, if he continued on that way, she'd be coming in no time. This wasn't what she had fantasized about. This wasn't how she wanted to orgasm.

Desperate for more, she grabbed the locks of hair that his mask didn't cover and dragged his head back. "I want your mouth on me. Right now. Your mouth. Your tongue. Eat me out. Make me come."

He yanked down her panties. Then his hand cupped her knee, and he hooked her leg over his shoulder before fitting his face between her thighs. His tongue skated over her pussy, and she gasped. Again and again, he licked her. Her pussy was so sensitive from her arousal that the lapping of his tongue coaxed out sighs.

His tongue traced the opening of her vagina.

Her body shook against the wall behind her.

The flimsy plywood rattled.

Laughter echoed throughout the haunted house.

She swiveled her head to the black curtain and caught glimpses of her friends walking past. Biting her bottom lip, she silenced the moans that wanted to slip free.

"Where's Sutton?" Mavis asked. "She would love this haunted house."

"I don't know," Travis said. "I thought she was waiting for us while we went on the zero-gravity ride."

Pumpkin Mask suddenly thrust her into the air and lifted her other leg over him so she now sat on his shoulders with his head firmly between her thighs.

She let out a laugh.

"Did you hear that?" Donna asked.

Their footsteps in the hallway stopped.

Pumpkin Mask fused his mouth around her pussy and set to work devouring her with her friends on the other side of the curtain.

Before she could clamp a hand over her mouth, a moan peeled out of her.

"Holy shit," Ralph said. "That was a woman moaning."

Her friends erupted into giggles.

"I think two scare actors are getting it on," Donna said.

"And I whole-heartedly approve," Trina said. "Get that D, girl!"

Their laughter grew.

Pumpkin Mask became empowered by her friends talking about them and feasted more sloppily, more ravenously.

She moaned into her palm.

"Let's move on," Trina said.

Sutton would thank Trina later for escorting their friends away. The moment she couldn't hear them anymore, she dropped her hand and wound her fingers through his locks, holding his head in place. She leaned her own head back against the plywood. All she could do was sink into the sensation of him consuming her. He ate her as if he could swallow her pussy.

"Oh God, yes, you're so good at that. So good."

Her words spurred him on even more than her friend's words.

Moans floated out of her throat.

A movement out of the corner of her eye drew her attention from his head wedged between her thighs to a man with a skull mask who had just entered their hiding place. The slurping sounds of Pumpkin Mask going down on her drew the other man's gaze to where Pumpkin Mask knelt. Something about this man being there, catching them, witnessing the carnality of it all urged a cry forth.

The man's head jerked up. "Fuck. Is he eating you out?" His voice was familiar. He was the one who had called her *baby girl* and was the first to leave when Pumpkin Mask showed up.

"Yes, he is."

He gawked.

She moaned.

Pumpkin Mask didn't so much as pause in his mission to make her come.

"And he's doing a damn fine job of it."

Pumpkin Mask's tongue located her clit and expertly toyed with it.

Her thighs clenched. Her legs shook. She grasped his head with both of her hands now. Another cry peeled out of her.

"Can I stay and watch?" the man asked.

She was about to say she didn't care if he did when Pumpkin Mask tore his mouth from her pussy. "Leave." His voice was a rasp that sent a shudder through her. The second he issued the order, he resumed his task and sucked her swollen clit into his mouth.

A long moan left her.

Skull Mask was still there, though.

"He told you to leave. If you make him stop again, I will hurt you."

"Damn it." Skull Mask left with a bulge in his pants and curses on his lips.

Pumpkin Mask's fingers dug into her thighs as he treated her pussy like an all-you-can-eat buffet. Now, she couldn't swallow her moans, even if she tried. She didn't care who heard her. She wanted them all to hear her cries as he made her pussy shatter with his clever, curious tongue and soft, supple lips.

Unable to stay still, she rolled her hips against his face.

Her pleasure expanded.

"Don't stop, don't stop. I'm so close."

She pumped her hips faster.

His mouth sucked harder.

"Yes, yes, yes."

Hot, tingling sparks of pleasure burned in her core.

"Oh God, oh God."

Her orgasm blasted through her body in a tidal wave of shimmering heat.

His tongue slicked gentle circles over her clit, stretching out her orgasm.

Finally, when nothing was left, she collapsed against the plywood.

His mouth left her aching pussy, and he eased her to her feet.

He stood with the mask still curled up over his mouth and nose. He had light stubble on his jawline and sexy lips swollen from eating her. She couldn't resist those lips as she grabbed his face and yanked his mouth to hers. Her flavor was all over his lips, and she didn't mind it. In fact, it heightened her hunger. Their kiss was all tongue and lips, all heat and lust.

When they parted, they were breathless.

"That was amazing," she said.

His mouth tilted up.

Seeing that smile heightened her desire to know the rest of his face. She began peeling the rubber mask up his cheeks, but before she could expose his features, he grabbed her wrists and lowered her hands. Shackling both of her wrists with one of his large hands, he worked his mask into place, hiding his strong jawline, dark blond stubble, and kissable lips.

She frowned. "We just went down on each other and I can't see your face?"

He didn't respond.

"Fine." She snatched up her panties and shorts, shook them out, and dragged them on. "I guess I was just the night's conquest after all."

She planned to leave him with those parting words, but he stole her arm, tugging her to a stop. Before she could snap, he evaporated all the words from her mouth when he cupped her face with his hands. He was breathing hard and shaking his head vigorously.

"Then why can't I see your face? And why won't you talk to me?"

He still didn't give her an answer.

"Then it's all an act then, isn't it?"

He shook his head slowly.

A *ding* sounded.

Her phone lay on the floor, glowing with a text. "I have to…" She shoved him out of the way to pluck up her phone.

A text from Trina waited.

> **Trina:** Where the hell are you?

Sutton tapped on the screen to reply back.

> **Sutton:** I'll meet you at the ticket booths. I'm ready to leave.

"I have to go."

She attempted to leave again, but he stilled her once more. Then he stole her phone from her fingers. He shifted so she could see him saving a new contact. Once he was finished, he showed her the screen.

"Lark," she read.

Before he passed her phone back, he did something else. Another *ding* sounded, but it wasn't her phone.

She took her device to see he'd texted himself nothing more than her name. "Is this you saying you'll call me some time?"

He dipped his head in a nod. Then he tweaked her chin. He did nothing else but that before he disappeared through the black curtain that led to the backstage of the haunted house.

Alone, she leaned into the plywood. What am I doing? She didn't know. All she knew for certain was that she wanted to get to know Lark. Would he ever let her see him maskless? She hoped so because she wanted him to see her without her masks.

5

Nyxie the Joker

*L*ark didn't remove his mask until he was in his truck after the park closed for the night. He gripped the steering wheel and rested his head back. Eyes closed, he thought about Sutton—his beautiful, scarred angel whose smile knotted his stomach and whose pussy tasted so damn good. He wanted her beyond tonight. Someone he just met, who had gotten under his skin so swiftly.

He dug his phone out of his pocket and brought up her name in his contacts. His fingers tapped the screen. Two words was all he yearned to tell her. Two little words. So, he sent the text.

> **Lark:** Goodnight, Sutton.

Three little dots appeared.

> **Sutton:** Night, Lark.

Her reply relieved him.

He drove to his little apartment in the heart of Orlando. His golden retriever Stella, who understood sign language, hand gestures, and finger snaps, bounded over with enthusiastic tail wags. When he had named Stella, he got a real kick out of it. Stella was a legendary name meant to be yelled at the top of your lungs, and here he couldn't so much as produce anything above a whisper. He had created a sign name for her, rather than spell out each letter, and he used it now, finishing with signing "yell" as a joke as if he were yelling her name.

Stella barked with joy.

Smiling, he rubbed her all over.

After getting all the doggy love, he showered and stood in front of the bathroom mirror.

Staring into his brown eyes, he practiced saying Sutton's name over and over. He didn't quit until he could fully whisper her name. The problem with that was, come morning, his throat hurt like hell. Even swallowing was difficult. He had to hold his throat, with his fingers on either side of his esophagus, in order to swallow just a sip.

Frustrated with the pain, the damage, the setback,

he popped a couple of pain relievers, wrapped a skinny heating pad around his neck, and hunkered behind his computer to work on his commissions. Nights, he had fun at All Horrors' Eve. Days, he created digital art to bring character sketches and cover art to life. Romance authors were his biggest clientele. It probably helped that he mixed in photos and videos of All Horrors' Eve into his content. The thirst traps attracted them, but his artwork kept them. Neither he nor his followers had any shame. He knew what he was doing, and so did they.

After twenty minutes of the heating pad, he swapped it for an ice pack with Velcro. Back and forth he did that, every twenty minutes. Not much could help when his vocal cords were acting up, but he did what he could, which included sipping ginger and lemon tea, although the pain had nothing to do with a sore throat like which came with a cold. Still, he fixed himself another cup and massaged his throat while taking a sip.

As he worked, Sutton sprang into his head. He created sketches for a client, and she was there in his thoughts the entire time. Her smell, her scent, her voice, her taste. Everything about her clung to him.

During his lunchbreak, he sent her a text.

> **Lark:** I can't stop thinking about you.

He set his phone down and replaced it with a ladle spoon. With his vocal cords acting up, his lunch consisted of noodles with plenty of broth.

Ding.

His gaze shifted to his phone's screen.
Her response had him sitting up straighter.

> **Sutton:** I can't stop thinking about you...

He dropped the spoon and replaced it with his phone to text back.

> **Lark:** I want to see you again.

He stared at the screen, waiting.
The three dots appeared. Then disappeared.
He debated over begging. Fortunately, he didn't have to. Her text came through.

> **Sutton:** So do I. Our haunted house is opening tonight. Why don't you come by? See what I do?

The text was accompanied with a promo flyer for Haunted House of Raunch's grand opening for the season. A few scare actors were pictured, and she was one of them. She wore a black and orange wig. Her makeup was done up to portray a sexy, chaotic joker, and her scar was visible. That makeup, paired with the skimpy checkered dress and orange corset, and holy shit he understood why people wanted to fuck scare actors in their costumes, because he wanted to bang her just like that. He fired back a response.

> **Lark:** I'll be there, angel.

> **Sutton:** Angel?

He grinned.

> **Lark:** That's right.

> **Sutton:** I'm no angel. You'll see

Her response intrigued him.

> **Lark:** No matter what you tell me or show me, you'll still be my angel.

> **Sutton:** Okay, stop.

Oh, but he couldn't. Teasing her was too much fun.

Lark: Are you blushing, sweetheart?

Sutton: Maybe.

The urge to see her flared stronger.

Lark: Send me a picture.

Sutton: To get off to?

Lark: Sure.

Sutton: I'm not sending you a picture unless you send me one.

Damn it. He should've guessed she'd want the same in return. No, he wasn't disfigured or anything. Rather, he liked to hide behind his mask...his computer screen...his phone's screen. Whatever mask he could put on, he did, because with a mask, he could be anyone. He didn't have to be a partial mute. Instead, he could be the silent stalker at All Horrors' Eve. No one had to know he was disabled when he wore one of his many masks. If he sent her a picture of himself as he was in this moment, it'd be him. No, his disability wouldn't be visible—no one could see it—but it'd still be him, and he tended to hide. Even in plain sight.

So, the text he sent came from his alter ego.

> **Lark:** The only picture you'll get of me, sweetheart, is of my cock.

The three little dots didn't appear, but panic did.

> **Lark:** Did I scare you off?

Those dots manifested, and he sighed.

> **Sutton:** You still don't scare me.

> **Lark:** That's good.

He wasn't sure if she'd continue their conversation when another text came.

> **Sutton:** If you want a picture of me, you'll have to drop trou.

you'll have to drop trou.

Her response blazed through his veins with a surge of lust. He pushed back from the table. His cock was already hard, so when he dragged down his zipper, he pulled it out and pointed his phone. The camera app made the classic shutter clicking sound as it captured an image of his cock in his fist. He sent it immediately. Gripping his cock, he waited.

Sutton: Wow. No foreplay? Are you always hard?

He chuckled.

Lark: I got hard seeing you as your joker character. Fucking sexy.

Sutton: That's Nyxie, daughter of Nyx, Goddess of the Night, born of chaos. You'll meet her tonight.

The promise of that had him syncing the ad to his computer so he could blow up the image of her as her joker alter ego. With the phone aimed at his cock, and his gaze glued to the image, he activated video recording and pumped his fist.

He imagined his hand was her pussy gripping his cock with the goal of milking him dry. God, he wanted the real thing. After catching glimpses of her pussy in the darkness of their hiding spot, after tasting her flesh and cum, he craved more. The need to be buried balls deep in her was fierce. Sure, he'd been desperate to be inside a woman before, but not like this. Nothing like this.

His grip tightened, and a groan rumbled in his throat. Further damage, but whatever. With the way he was headed, he'd likely shatter his vocal cords from an orgasm. In the moment, though, he didn't give a fuck. He worked his fist up and down.

He thought about that joker-smile painted mouth of hers wrapped around his cock. Would she let him stroke the head of his cock over her scar? Decorate it with his cum? He circled the pad of his thumb over the tip, imagining his cock's head was her skin, her scar. Pre-cum leaked forth. His thumb swirled faster.

He continued to study the photo. That little joker skirt around smooth, tan thighs. Shit. He yearned to fit his head between her strong thighs again. Better yet, he'd grip those pretty thighs, lift her onto his lap, and have her sink his cock into her depths. Eyelids squeezed tight, he held that image in his mind. She was there now, warming his lap, lifting herself against him, riding him to climax.

His hand became erratic.

His moans were strained.

He came all over his hand.

Panting, he ended the recording. Without another thought, he sent it.

Fifteen minutes later, he received a photo. Sutton's head was on a pillow. Her black, feathery hair was mussed around her head. A flush stained her cheeks and chest. Light glimmered in her eyes. Her lips were parted slightly. If he was right, she'd just orgasmed, and nothing was more stunning.

He tapped out a text.

> **Lark:** You're so damn beautiful. Are you in bed?

> **Sutton:** I just climaxed to your video. Thanks for that.

He liked knowing she got off to his video.

> **Lark:** You're welcome, but the next time you come, it'll be on my cock. And that's a vow.

He imagined her blushing and wished he were there to see it.

> **Sutton:** See you tonight?

He drew in a deep breath.

Lark: Tonight.

And, shit, he didn't know how he'd wait that long.

He did the only thing he could to try to get his mind off her and resumed working. His lunch was long forgotten now.

Hours later, a knock lured him away from his work and his distracting thoughts of Sutton. He checked through the peephole to see his sister. Amy was five years younger than him but since his accident, she'd cared for him as though she were the oldest sibling.

He opened the door. "Hey, sis," he mouthed and signed.

She elevated onto tiptoe to kiss him on the cheek. Whenever she spoke, even though she didn't need to, she also signed to him. "Hey, bro. You need to shave."

He gave a voiceless laugh. "The ladies love the stubble."

"Oh, I'm sure." She pointed at her neck. "What's wrong?"

"What is usually wrong. I strained my crappy vocal cords. It's fine."

She pursed her lips. "It's not fine. I hate seeing you in pain."

He framed her face with his hands and planted a kiss in the middle of her forehead. Then he lowered his hands to sign. "I'll be okay. I promise."

"I can't help but worry about you. You hole up in

here and only go out to do your spooky shit, and probably only hook up with the women who go to the park looking for a good time."

He grimaced and laid his palms together. "Please." His hands signed quickly. "I do not need my little sister thinking about me hooking up with anyone."

"Okay, well, ew, it's not like I want to. I just—"

He caught her hand. With his free hand, he signed, "I met someone."

"Oh my God. When?"

"Last night."

"You mean at the park? Seriously, Lark?"

"She's different. She has a scar." He traced a line across his neck.

"Oh my God." Horror reflected on her face.

He glared. "Don't do that. Don't you dare do that. She's beautiful."

"I'm sorry. Okay? I'm sorry. How did she get the scar? Do you know?"

"She had open thyroid surgery to remove tumors."

"Does she have the ability to speak?"

"Yes."

"Does she know that *you* can't speak?"

He exhaled, knowing exactly what would happen next. "No."

"Why the hell not? Come on, Lark, you can't keep it a secret from everyone."

Anger came swift. "I'm not! The people who matter know. Family knows, my friends from high school know, and my favorite barista knows ASL."

"So, *she* doesn't matter?"

He clenched his jaw a moment before mouthing

with his hand motions. "That's not what I meant. She matters, which is why I haven't told her yet."

"That doesn't make sense."

"It does! Look, I don't have to wear a fucking sign around my neck or a name tag that says, 'Hi, my name is Lark. My vocal cords are fucked up from a car accident that left them mostly paralyzed, so I can't speak. What's your name?'"

"That's not what I meant, and you know that. After your accident, you stopped dating. You have one-night stands, but this girl, she seems like she would understand. You, yourself, said she was different."

"And she is."

"Then tell her."

Frustration had him sweeping the forgotten bowl of soup off the table. It smacked into the wall, spraying noodles everywhere, and clattered to the floor. "Don't fucking pressure me to do something that I'm not fucking ready to do!"

Amy took a step back, clearly startled by his outburst, and he despised himself for causing that. She rubbed her fist in slow circles over her heart. "I'm sorry."

Shaking his head, he grasped her shoulders and mouthed, "*I'm* sorry."

"I told you...I just worry about you. I don't mean to be pushy."

He ran a hand down her hair and lifted his free hand. "I know."

She sighed. "You should put some Vicks on your neck. It might help."

"I will when I go to bed. I'm seeing Sutton tonight.

I don't want to smell like medicated rub."

Amy laughed. Then she became serious. "Wait. Her name is Sutton?"

"Yeah."

"That's a hot name."

He grinned. "Stop."

She grinned back. "And you're seeing her tonight?"

"Yeah."

"Where?"

He showed her the ad on his phone.

"The two of you are going to a haunted house for your first date? After meeting at a Halloween theme park? That's a little too cliché."

"It's not a cliché if she works there."

Amy's eyes widened. "No way."

"She's the joker."

Amy leaned closer to get a better view of the photo. "Damn. She *is* hot."

"Okay. That's enough." He locked the screen and stashed his phone. "I don't need my sister checking out my girl."

"Oh, she's your girl already?"

He smirked, recalling the conversation from last night with Sutton. "She is."

Amy glanced at the bowl on the floor and Stella slurping up the noodles. "You didn't eat lunch." She set down her purse. "Sit. Stella's got the mess handled, and I'm going to make you an omelet. You're going to need your strength when you see Sutton tonight."

He smiled. "An omelet sounds good."

Seeing Sutton tonight sounded even better.

6

Haunted House of Raunch

Sutton wanted to be sure Haunted House of Raunch was ready for opening night, so she did a walk-through. In the beginning, they didn't have the traditional graveyard like many, but a pitch-black space punctuated by a flashing strobe light. The moment she stepped through, men dropped from the rafters lining the alleyway. They wore full tactical gear from head to toe, complete with knee pads and bulletproof vests. Masks and night-vision goggles covered their faces.

"What are you doing here, sweetheart?" one of them said, his voice distorted and deep.

"Are you looking for us?" another said.

"We can show you pain."

"We can show you pleasure."

They stepped closer.

Ah, shit. She wasn't supposed to get turned on already, but she was. Although Haunted House of Raunch was her creation and she knew each segment's theme, the rest was up to the scare actors for that section, so she had no idea what they had up their sleeves. She definitely didn't expect them to talk about pain and pleasure.

"Think you can handle all of us, baby girl?"

At least they'd taken her tip about calling their guests *baby girl*. That would definitely wet several panties a night.

"You might want to leave while you still can."

"But we can't let her leave."

"She's ours now."

"All ours."

"And we're not going to share her."

"No, we're not."

They came closer.

Suddenly, a chainsaw revved behind her, and she found their largest scare actor blocking her way. He leaned in close to whisper, "Run, little mouse."

She turned back to find the men in full tactical gear had vanished.

The giant scare actor was meant to drive the guests to the next segment of the haunted house. He bore down on her, taking step by step. Menacing. Threatening. A dark force to scare and excite.

She entered the next section to find a filthy, grimy alley.

A man was being murdered by three men right in

the middle of that alley. He screamed, and his fright echoed off the walls. The killers plunged a knife into their victim's body. Blood sprayed into the air, splattering them. The change from the men in tactical gear teasing to this was startling. From arousal to terror. It was perfect.

The killers looked up and glared with murderous intent.

A woman, holding her stomach as blood poured over her hands, staggered out in the open. "Run!"

Suddenly, a group of people rushed out in a stampede of wounds and gushing blood. They herded her to the next part of the haunted house—a prison replica with scare actors behind real iron bars. A half-naked man with bulging muscles and tattoos covering his chest and back performed pull-ups right in front of his door, letting everyone who would stop there get a good look at his ripped body. While she couldn't help but stare at his crotch, which was right in front of her face as he lifted himself up and down, hands came into her peripheral.

She twisted around.

The man in the cell behind her wore a leather mask. He attempted to grab her again, and she headed down the skinny aisle.

In the next cell, a man was chained up. His arms were above his head, and a woman in a skimpy guard costume whipped him in a way clearly meant to arouse.

Sutton bit her bottom lip. A little BDSM in a haunted house? Why not? She happened to know that the scare actor getting whipped got off on it. He'd probably have to jerk off in one of their secret spaces between every few groups of guests.

In the cell beside that one, Donna was strapped to a chair, trying to break free. She wore an orange jumpsuit with strategic rips meant to showcase her amazing rack and toned abs. Her gaze landed on Sutton. She fought harder against her restraints and let out a yell that bounced off the cells.

Sutton continued on. Each cell after that, the prisoners advanced in their degree of unhinge. Men in solitary confinement. Women in straitjackets. In the final cell, a man stood in the middle of the fake cement with his back to her. A straitjacket confined his arms. He circled around slowly to reveal blood gushing down his chin and neck and staining his teeth.

The segment after the prison was her domain...or Nyxie's domain. This was where she'd select a lucky participant from each group, sit them down in a chair, taunt them with fake strands of intestine, handcuff them to the chair, and give them a psychotic lap dance. Yup, their haunted house did what other haunted houses did not. Scare actors *could* touch guests, if guests agreed before walking through the entrance, but guests could not touch them. Hence, the cuffs. If there wasn't a willing participant in the group, they'd plant a couple of their own for these purposes, who would act the part and who they could trust.

After her act, they increased the sex appeal.

A coven of witches, led by Mavis, in the next segment would choose someone as a sacrifice. Since she was the only one to choose from, they laid her down on a table, wrapped a thin rope around her hands, leaving it untied, and stroked her arms and legs in worshiping ways. She squirmed from their touch. The witches chanted, which only made the whole thing hotter. There would be many boners and wet pussies on that table. Hers was only the first.

In the height of it, Mavis raised an athame high and thrust it down. The fake blade retracted when it touched Sutton's chest. The witches shrieked with crazed laughter, and fake blood, from a clever hidden button, shot out in all directions. Mavis raised a rubber heart dripping with red, as if she'd just hacked it from Sutton's chest.

With the heart in the air, the other guests would be chased out of there.

Sutton climbed off the table. "Shit, ladies," she whispered. "I'm creeped out *and* horny."

They grinned.

After them, came Trina in her sexy gauzy dress, white wig, and boobs galore. But she didn't reveal herself right away. Wondering where Trina was hiding, Sutton walked through a dead garden full of withered flowers, black roses, spider webs, and trees bearing rotten fruit. Sutton was passing a tree of blackened apples when Trina emerged from behind the trunk.

She wore a gauzy white and gray dress that showed off her fabulous rack. Her chest was dusted with white powder. The crease between her perfectly round breasts glittered. Her lips were blood-red, her eyes layered with black for a haunted look, and her white wig stretched down her back. She portrayed a trampy banshee to a tee and usually had countless people who stepped foot into Haunted House of Raunch fantasizing about making her scream their names.

Trina let out a hideous cry that sent chills down Sutton's spine.

One by one, more banshees appeared, adding their screams to Trina's, creating a beautifully terrifying chorus. The way they advanced, staring and shrieking, could induce anxiety. Sutton felt it clawing up her back and tightening her own throat.

She passed through the decaying curtain to an empty stretch of darkness.

A light flashed.

Nothing.

The light flashed again.

She caught sight of one of the men from the beginning in full tactical gear standing at the end of the hall. When the light flashed again, he was closer.

Another flash.

Gone.

Flash.

Now two.

Flash.

Gone.

Flash.

Three.

Flash.

Gone.

On and on until she counted six of them.

Flash.

Gone.

She didn't know what they had planned next.

Flash.

One. Right in front of her face.

Flash.

Gone.

Then a roaring chainsaw behind her made her flinch.

That chainsaw was meant to get everyone running out of the haunted house, so she exited, bursting with pride. Haunted House of Raunch was creepy as hell and sexy as fuck. This was exactly what she had hoped for, and they all delivered.

She praised her crew and complimented each group. "There's a lot of scary shit going on in our country these days, and it's our job to be scary right back. This haunted house is our protest in a time when romance books with any level of sex are being targeted, pleasure is called sinful, women's rights are being ripped away and women are reduced to nothing more than their ovaries, love and relationships different from the traditional are deemed wrong, and people who disagree and fight back are being forced out or are getting locked up. This haunted house is an escape for the people needing healthy fear and a place of permission for them to enjoy the things that scare and arouse them."

Her crew nodded.

"Tonight is opening night, so let's give it our all."

The first guests arrived forty-five minutes before they opened their doors. Outside, the line was long. Scare actors kept them entertained with taunts. By the time the groups arrived at Sutton's station, she could tell they were excited in many ways. She went through her act, mixing it up each time so it wouldn't become stale or boring, using the people's reactions for a cue.

The third group of people left, and she prepped for

the fourth group.

Donna's screams tipped Sutton off that they were close.

She got into position.

The first guest stepped over the threshold.

She let out her first maniacal giggle and pinned her gaze on him. Behind him the other guests filtered in. She did her little jerking sways as if she were a broken wind-up doll. The final person stepped into her domain, and she jolted to a stop, almost breaking character, because that person was Lark in his black cargo pants, leather vest, and pumpkin mask.

When it came time to select her victim, she pretended to consider the options before her. She stopped in front of Lark. "You think you're a tough guy?" She swayed. "Let's see how tough." She gripped his vest, yanked him out of the lineup, and shoved him onto the wooden chair.

She went through her skit, towing bloody sausage links from a fake torso on a dinner table and draping them around Lark's shoulders. The others grimaced and backed away and were obviously disgusted, but Lark didn't flinch. From her gruesome feast spread out on the table, she picked up a severed rubber finger and licked it from base to tip.

"Oh my gosh. So gross," a young woman said.

Laughing, she trailed the corpse finger up Lark's arm. "Do you wanna play?"

His brown eyes flashed up, and she knew he did. He wanted to play.

She slapped cuffs on each of Lark's wrists to shackle his hands to the chair's legs and performed a teasing lap dance with more fake organs as props. At the end, she removed a plastic knife from her boot and leveled it to his throat. Compressing a hidden button, she slashed her arm out, pretending to slit his throat. Fake blood squirted out of the tip of the blade.

The guests yelped in horror and fled.

Once alone, Sutton let out a soft giggle. "That always gets them." She straddled his lap. "Now we can really play." With the tip of the fake blade, she traced a tic-tac-toe game on his chest.

The handcuffs rattled.

"Nuh-huh. You're mine. I get to do what I want with you now, and you don't need hands for what I want to do." She ground into him.

He inhaled sharply.

So, he still wasn't going to speak? That was alright. She didn't need him to say a word to indicate that he was turned on, because she was rubbing against his erection. Proof enough.

"Usually, I do my little dance, but I don't do this." She twined her arms around his neck that was still adorned by the bloody sausage links. "I don't grind on anyone's lap, but your lap is far too tempting."

His chest heaved up and down as he breathed deeply.

She maintained her grinding motion. "You don't know anything about me. I don't know anything about you. But this is just too good. What we have. What we do know of each other…it's just too good to resist. Isn't it?"

He nodded.

"I know it is." She pinched the rubber edge of his

mask.

He jerked his head back.

She stilled. "Trust me." Careful not to cross his boundaries, she peeled the mask up to the tip of his nose. She ran her fingertips down the stubble on his cheeks. "You have a beautiful mouth." And she rubbed her lips over his.

He leaned forward to claim her mouth, but she inched back. When he stretched more, she stayed out of his reach. He jerked on the cuffs. His desperation to kiss her excited her. Laying her lips finally to his, she let him feast. He kissed her as if famished. As if they hadn't devoured each other last night. As if they would never get the chance to taste each other again. And although he wasn't touching her with his hands, he still managed to have her melting into him. That was what he could do. With just his lips. His mouth was magical.

She broke their kiss. "If I release you, will you be a good boy?"

He snorted.

"Is that a no? Are you going to be naughty?"

His hips lifted.

She gasped. "Naughty it is. I'm going to release you, but—" With a grip on his hair, she jerked his head back. "I run this show, got it?"

He nodded.

"Good." She removed the keys from her pocket and opened the cuffs.

The second he was freed, his right hand lifted as quick as elastic snapping into place. She caught his hand before he could grab the back of her head and tug her in for a kiss that she knew would be devastatingly amazing.

"I. Run. This. Show. Or have you forgotten already?"

His lips twitched, but the smile failed to grow, because his gaze shifted to her hand. Or, more precisely, to her left wrist. She knew it without having to look, because of the simple fact that his smile faltered and faded. Confirmation came when his thumb grazed over the inside of her wrist and the vertical scar there.

"Ladies and gentleman—" She knocked her head from side to side. "He's discovered my other scar."

His gaze flicked to hers. The tenderness there shocked her.

The sassiness of Nyxie dropped away. "Like the one that graces my neck, I don't hide it. This one, though, isn't as innocent. I was sixteen. Stupid. I tried to end it all, because I thought my heartbreak was worth ending it all for. I was young. I was stupid. I was wrong."

He cradled her wrist with his hand, brought it to his lips, and pressed a soft kiss to her scar that had once marked heartbreak.

"Lark." Tears blurred her vision. "You like my scars, don't you?"

He embraced her head with his hands and leaned forward. One word was all he said, and it was a breath of a whisper that filled her with hope. "Love."

She needed him. Now.

Frantic, she attacked his pants, popping the button and dragging down the zipper. She dipped her hand inside and drew out his cock—thick and veined and beautiful. Her pussy throbbed.

He slipped his hand into his pocket and extracted a condom.

She took it. "Are you clean?"

Nod.

"I trust you. I'm clean, and I'm on the pill. Do you trust me?"

Nod.

"Then I want you raw." And she flicked the condom behind him. Then she scrambled to her feet, yanked her panties over her boots, and chucked them onto the dinner table. Back on his lap, she leveled over him. She sank onto him, letting his cock stretch her. "Oh God." Grasping his shoulders, she lowered even more until he filled her completely. "Jesus, you feel so good." And she rocked into him.

"Mm." His hands clutched her, and he tugged her forward. He copied the motion of her hips, hoisting her up and down his length.

Arms tied around his neck, she pumped away. She moaned as his cock stroked every bit of sensitive flesh. Being restricted to the small space of the chair didn't mean a thing. She rode him with vigor, and he encouraged her to go faster with his strong grip on her hips.

Warmth pooled inside her. A glittering sensation spread from her clit to her abdomen. It swirled inside her, growing bigger and brighter. She couldn't slow, couldn't be sure Lark would follow her, because her orgasm was already coming. A cry broke from her when her orgasm shattered. She held onto him tightly as her muscles contracted.

Lark's fingers dug into her. He rammed into her, plunging deep. One of his hands disappeared from her hip. A muted rumbling met her ears. More warmth filled her, but this time it was his cum.

She moaned, knowing that he was giving her every drop of himself.

Heart racing, she rested against him.

His hands caressed her back.

She wanted nothing more than to cuddle there on that rickety chair, but Donna's scream jolted Sutton to reality. "Shit." She climbed off him and lifted the fake intestines from his shoulders. "The next group is coming."

He stood and fixed his pants. Then he laid a palm to her cheek. Unspoken words passed between them from a connection she'd never had with anyone else.

She flattened her hand to his. "I know. Now, go."

He slipped from the room to continue on.

Legs still shaking from her orgasm, she scurried behind the table. Lark's cum leaked down the inside of her thighs. It made her joker's smile wider as the next group entered her domain.

7

Books & Brews

ark drove to All Horrors' Eve, and even though he knew Sutton was working, he couldn't help but look for her among the guests that night. Or the next night. Or the next. They texted throughout the day, but messages weren't enough. He craved her constantly, and not just her body, but simple contact, like their texts. They hadn't discussed when they'd see each other again after he hustled out of the haunted house so she wouldn't get caught screwing around, but he was desperate to see her again, to hear her voice, to taste more of her body.

Wednesday morning, he received a text from his boss that one of the rides was down and they needed him to check it out, because aside from doing the park's promo posters and being a scare actor, he was also their only mechanic. Cheaper that way.

He texted back.

> **Lark:** I'll be there in an hour.

Smelling of the medicated rub he'd applied to his throat when he woke up, he left to hit the local coffee shop for book lovers before heading to the park. He frequented Books & Brews on specific days because he knew his favorite barista would be there. The first time she served him coffee, he'd been amazed when he'd pointed to his order on the menu and she'd replied back with sign language. He'd never had that before. Not at any coffee shop or restaurant. Being able to talk to someone in customer service who could understand him was a relief. Plus, she made damn good beverages.

He walked into the little shop.

Benny peered over her shoulder as she made someone's latte. Beaming her wattage smile, she waved.

Waving back, he joined the line to wait his turn.

Benny perked up when he stepped up to the counter. "Hey, how is my favorite customer this morning?" She didn't talk when she signed, so no one else, unless they knew ASL, would know what they were saying. Unless they could read lips, because she mouthed her words just like he did.

"I'm good. Better than good, actually."

"Oh, are you getting laid?"

He chuckled on a breath. "You could say that."

"It's about damn time." She grinned. "Do you want

your usual?"

"Not today. I'd love one of your miracle healing teas, though." She made the best damn tea. They were like magic.

She tilted her head. "Are you feeling okay?"

He shrugged a shoulder while she input his order on the computer. "Yeah, just the same problematic vocal cords. No big deal."

"I'll make my best tea just for you. Have a seat. I'll have it done in a moment."

"Thank you." He sat at a table. While he waited, he scrolled through Sutton's social media and admired her beauty from afar. He inhaled, taking in the fragrance of coffee beans and the sweetness of baked goods. How he wished he was smelling the lovely scent of her perfume instead. He didn't know what notes made up her fragrance, but he loved it. Her scent was heavenly. Infinitely better than coffee.

He continued to scroll and frowned when he realized that she hid her scar in a lot of her pictures. Her selfies either cut off before it or her hair covered it. She shouldn't have to hide her scar. Her scar was beautiful, and if he could, he'd shout that to the world.

"Lark."

He retrieved the to-go cup from Benny.

"Taste it. Let me know your thoughts."

He sipped. The flavors exploded on his tongue. And yet, they were comforting. He swallowed. The tea slid down as if embracing his throat from the inside. "Holy crap," he signed. "That's incredible." He tapped his card to the reader.

Benny handed him a tiny baggie with handles.

"Something sweet. On the house."

"Thank you." He accepted it.

"Take care of yourself."

"You, too."

He backed away from the counter just as the bell over the door jingled. His gaze lifted, and he jolted as if struck. His scarred angel was entering the shop where he purchased his coffee a few times a week. She walked toward him, and he stopped breathing. There could be no way she'd recognize him. No way. He'd worn a mask. He didn't have tattoos or scars or birth marks. The stubble on his jaw, maybe the hair on the back of his head—that was about all she'd seen. Well, aside from his chest and cock, but he was fully clothed now. She couldn't tell him apart from any other stranger in a coffee shop. It'd be impossible.

Still, he froze.

That smile of hers graced her pretty lips. And she was aiming it right at him. In the real world.

He managed a smile in return. Instead of continuing to the door, he changed direction and sat at a table. She spoke to Benny as if she was a regular. Benny even knew her preferred drink without needing to be told. They chatted at the counter while Benny crafted Sutton's coffee. Sutton's laughter met his ears, and he wished she was joking with him.

Benny handed Sutton her coffee. Then, with a quick wink, she slid over a bag identical to the one he held.

Sutton smiled. "Thank you. You're the best." She carried her coffee and free goodie over to the table diagonal to his and sat facing him.

He pulled out his cell phone and pretended to be looking at it while stealing peeks at her.

She sipped. Foam lingered on her lip. Her tongue darted out to clean the white foam from her upper lip, and his stomach clenched.

Wanting to talk to her but being a complete coward, he opened their texts. He wrote out a message. Looking at her, he sent it.

Lark: Good morning, beautiful. What are you up to?

She leaned forward to peer at her phone lying on the tabletop. A smile wider than the one she'd given him a moment ago appeared on her face. She plucked up her phone. Her nails clicked softly as she tapped out a reply.

His phone vibrated in his hand.

Sutton: I'm having coffee at this cute little shop. Books & Brews. Have you ever been?

Lark: I have.

Sutton: We could've been here at the same time and never knew it.

He glanced over, but her gaze was latched onto her screen.

> **Lark:** That's possible.

She peered around the shop.

He feigned interest in his phone and tapped out a text so she would look at her screen.

> **Lark:** When can I see you again?

She bit her bottom lip.

> **Sutton:** Today?

He stole a glimpse.

> **Lark:** You're not working?

> **Sutton:** I'm off from my admin job. I have time to kill before I have to go to the haunted house.

> **Lark:** I'm actually going to the park to work on a ride. It broke down. Could you meet me there in 2 hours?

> down. Could you meet me there
> in 2 hours?

She nodded and mouthed "yes," but sent him a different reply.

> **Sutton:** You repair the rides, too?

> **Lark:** I'm a helpful guy.

She let out a small snort.

> **Sutton:** Will security let me in?

> **Lark:** I'll leave your name with them. Any time you want to come, you can.

She flattened a hand to her cheek as a flush crept over it.

He grinned at her gutter mind and texted back what he hoped would get the flush to cover her entire body.

> **Lark:** That wasn't meant to be an innuendo, but I want to make you come again. I want my cock buried so deep inside that pretty pussy.

She cleared her throat and nudged her cup away. Her fingers were lightning fast on her phone.

> **Sutton:** Stop. I'm in public. This is scandalous.

He held back even a voiceless chuckle.

> **Lark:** You're lucky I'm not with you.

And there she went nibbling on her bottom lip again.

Suddenly, the screen on his phone changed to show she was calling him. She raised the phone to her ear.

Fuck, fuck, fuck, fuck. He sprang to his feet and jabbed the red button. As he left, he caught the disappointment that flickered across her face. Items in hand, he rushed out the door. On the sidewalk, he set his to-go cup and the little baggie on a brick ledge. Before he could text her back an excuse, she texted him.

> **Sutton:** I thought that if you wanted to have foreplay that we should hear each other.

Fuck! He frantically tapped out a reply.

> **Lark:** I'm sorry, baby, I can't talk.

How true those words were.

> **Lark:** Besides, you're in public, remember? How scandalous.

Through the window, he noticed her smile.

> **Sutton:** You're right.

He exhaled when her reply came through.

> **Sutton:** So...2 hours?

He gave a small nod.

> **Lark:** 2 hours, baby, and then you can pick a ride for us to fuck on.

Her eyes widened.

Grinning, he stashed his phone and headed to his truck.

At the park, he carried his mask to security. Usually, they just nodded their heads and let him pass, but this time he gave Dan, the head of the park's security, a folded piece of paper. On it, he'd written: *My girl Sutton is coming in a couple of hours. Make sure she gets access. Tell the others she's allowed in whenever she wants. No hassle.*

Dan bowed his head. "You've got it."

He signed, "Thank you" and continued on.

Mask in hand, he made his way through the grounds. He found Mitch, his boss, at the snow cone booth, flirting with the girl who manned it while the park was open and during the day while staff cared for the grounds, in case they needed something to cool down. Certainly appeared like Mitch needed to cool down with how heated things appeared between him and Steph.

Mitch noticed Lark approaching. He waved and, as the only person at the park who knew ASL, signed to Lark. "Hey, thank you for coming early."

Lark signed back. "No problem. Which ride failed?"

"The Himalaya."

Shit. Out of all the rides at the park, that ride could

not go down. The Himalaya was one of the most popular rides on the property.

"I'll get right on it." He took a step, but Mitch stopped him.

"What's with the mask? You know you don't have to wear that when the park is closed, right?"

"I have a guest coming and…" He paused. His next words would make him sound like an absolute weirdo. "Well, she doesn't know what I look like without my mask on. Right now, I'd like to keep it that way."

Mitch squinted. "Okay." He peered around. "You know what? I have an idea." He plucked a radio from his belt and lifted it to his lips. "When Lark's guest comes, broadcast it on the radios. Everyone on the property will then immediately put on their masks. No exceptions. Is that understood?"

"Affirmative."

"Yes, sir."

"Will do."

Everyone there said something similar.

Gratitude filled Lark. "Thank you."

Mitch nodded.

On his way to the Himalaya, he considered the rides there. So many opportunities to have fun with Sutton. He could suspend her from the swing ride, and, although the part of her body that he'd want to touch the most would be behind a barrier, he could caress every other inch of her body. His touch would have her quivering in that swing and the chains rattling.

He passed the Ferris wheel where he could have the operator stop them at the very top and he could have her sit on his lap. They'd shake that car every which way as she rode him with vigor. Hopefully she wasn't scared of heights.

Next to the Ferris wheel was the carousel. Instead of the traditional pretty horses, their carousal let visitors ride beasts and monsters—a werewolf, minotaur, dragon, basilisk, and centaur. He imagined her lying atop the centaur, with her head nestled at the centaur's neck. As the carousel rotated, he'd stand behind the centaur and pound into Sutton until she squirted all over him and the centaur's hindquarters. God, it'd be hot as fuck.

Liking the thought of that, he continued to the Himalaya. Once there, he activated the mechanism that would turn the ride on, but it just shuddered and made a hideous grinding sound. He deactivated the ride. Whatever was wrong, the problem was related to the track. He stripped out of his shirt so he wouldn't get it all sweaty and got to work. First, he checked the visible track. Everything looked fine. Then he turned the ride on and pushed the cars so he could see the track the ride hid. Grinding and clanking filled the air. The track he uncovered was also fine, albeit a little dinged. That meant something was stuck within the gears of the cars. Great. This wasn't a one-person job.

He texted Mitch and waited for a crew, including Cal, to meet him. They all had their masks, ready to put on once they received word that Sutton arrived. Together, they detached and removed the cars one by one so that Lark could inspect their underbellies. The first two cars were fine. The third car, though, had a one-inch drill bit wedged into the space where the track fit.

"The fuck," Cal said.

Lark snapped a picture of the bit and texted it to Mitch.

Mitch's text came right away.

> **Mitch:** How the fuck did that happen?

> **Lark:** I don't know. The ride would never have worked if we'd left it.

> **Mitch:** Get it out.

> **Lark:** Yes, sir.

Cal handed Lark a hammer.

He used the hammer to beat against one side of the bit. The racket echoed against his eardrums. The vibrations of each hit rattled up his arm to his shoulder. He struck the drill bit near the end again and again. It slid slightly. Hit after hit after hit. His teeth were on edge from the sound of the piece of metal scratching against more metal. Finally, the bit came loose and fell to the metal flooring with a clank. He picked it up and snapped a picture to send to Mitch.

Mitch responded with a thumbs-up emoji.

Lark, Cal, and the other crew members lifted the

car back onto the track. They had just reconnected all the cars when Dan's voice came over the walkie. "Sutton is incoming."

Mitch's voice broadcasted over the walkies next. "Masks on, everyone. We're doing this for our boy."

Cal shot Lark a grin before lowering his skull mask into place.

Lark slid his own mask over his face.

All around him, the other crew members did the same. Then they lined up in front of the Himalaya to see if the ride would work. Lark twisted the key switch and pressed the green button. The ride started up and ran beautifully.

"Lark?"

He turned, and so did everyone else.

Sutton jolted to a stop as she took them all in. "Um. Hi. So…the masks are mandatory?"

"That's right." Mitch stepped up beside her. "Whenever they step foot on park grounds, masks are required to keep up the mystery, even when we're closed." He held out a hand to Sutton. "I'm Mitch. I own and operate the park."

Sutton shook his hand. "Nice to meet you."

Mitch's gaze swept over her as he shook her hand. "You, too."

The fuck? Lark stepped up beside her, glaring at Mitch through the eyeholes of his mask.

Sutton withdrew her hand.

Mitch chuckled and nudged his chin at Lark. "You're in good hands, sweetheart." Then he glanced at the other guys, and he knocked his head to the side. "Let's leave these two to have their fun."

As the guys left, Sutton faced him.

Being face to face—or face to mask—with her after this morning, Lark couldn't restrain himself. He grabbed her while tugging his mask up and crushed his mouth to hers. The moment their lips touched, his craving only intensified. He grasped the backs of her thighs. Her body rubbed against his as he lifted her, and her legs instantly latched around his waist. They kissed with a clear hunger that he doubted would ever be sated.

Cheers and whistles flooded the air.

Sutton laughed against his mouth. "Your friends seem to approve."

He slid his hands to her butt and squeezed.

She shifted back. Her gaze lowered to his mouth, and she bit her bottom lip. The tips of her fingers traced the bottom of his mask.

He sensed she wanted to remove his mask but was holding herself back from crossing his unspoken boundary. To show her how much he appreciated that, he kissed her harder.

"Mm. You're an amazing kisser."

Well, he kinda had to be. Considering his lips were really only good for kissing and eating, he figured they should be skilled when it came to kissing and eating a woman's body.

He set her feet on the ground.

Arms still twined around his neck, she peered at her surroundings. "It looks different during the day."

He fixed his mask into place before taking her hand and leading her through the park so she could see everything in the light.

They didn't talk.

The way the sun reflected off her dark hair, lighting it up with red and purples was memorizing. Then her gaze was on his, and her emerald eyes were like gems between thick lashes.

"You know what you said about me picking a ride we can fuck on?"

He dipped his head.

"Funny enough, last night, I had this intense sex dream…we were on the zero-gravity ride."

Interesting. He hadn't considered that one.

"I'm actually terrified of that ride, but the dream was hot."

And that sealed it. They would fuck on the zero-gravity ride.

8

Zero Gravity Ride

*S*utton talked nervously as they strolled through the park. She'd been yapping so much that she hadn't realized where they were heading until she found herself staring at the zero-gravity ride. Lark was directing her toward the ramp. She dug her heels into the pavement and yanked on her hand. "Nonono. I was serious, Lark. This ride freaks me out. I can't get on that thing."

He faced her and laid a gentle hand to her cheek. Through the eyeholes of his mask, his gaze penetrated her. Calmness seeped into her from his touch and stare. He was asking her to trust him without voicing a single syllable. And for reasons she couldn't explain, she did trust him. He'd seen her at work and seen all her scars. What they had was so new, but she trusted him.

"Okay," she whispered.

He removed his phone from his pocket and tapped on the screen.

A moment later, a man in a skull mask appeared. She recognized his build and swagger. He was the man who'd shown Trina a good time and had called her *baby girl* in the cemetery's haunted house. He opened the door to the zero-gravity ride and waved a hand. "All aboard."

Hand in hand, Lark led her up the ramp.

Stepping inside the UFO-shaped contraption, the first dregs of anxiety hit her, but Lark squeezed her hand, giving her the courage to fully enter the ride. He led her to a padded panel against the wall on the other side of the doorway.

Heart racing, she leaned against the panel.

Lark peered over his shoulder, and Sutton saw Skull Mask getting into the operator's chamber set up in the center of the ride. The chair faced away from them. Lark's gaze met hers next and his fingers sought the button of her jeans. Her eyes widened, and she sucked in a breath. His intentions were obvious. He really did mean to fuck her on this ride.

She shivered as he drew her jeans down her legs. On his way back to his feet, he lifted his mask again and trailed kisses up her thighs. The final kiss was between her legs, directly over her clit. She bit her bottom lip. As he stood, he fixed his mask.

He folded her jeans, carried them to the operator's chamber, and passed them to Skull Mask. While made his way back, the tension in his body spoke volumes. When he stepped closer, she saw the heat burning in the opaqueness of his eyes. His needs radiated off him like solar flares. It left her parched and thirsty for however he could quench her.

In front of her, he dropped to his knees, cupped her hips with his hands, and went right to the task of getting her to relax, which he did by pinpointing her clit with the tip of his tongue. He rubbed her clit through the cotton of her panties, and the contact had her melting against the padded panel. She couldn't stop herself from gripping his hair at the back of his head. He teased her so exquisitely that he pried a moan out of her before she could silence it, knowing that Skull Mask was right there and could hear it.

Her moan clearly affected Lark. Instantly, his hands gripped her tighter. His fingertips dug into her ass, and he attacked her clit with vigor. The cry that left her then echoed throughout the enclosure.

"Oh, God, Lark." She rocked her hips against his face.

Her panties were damp from his tongue and her arousal when he shifted back. She damn-near whimpered, but then he was peeling those wet panties down, and she couldn't whimper at that, because she would be getting far more than teasing passes of his tongue over cotton.

He stood and stuffed her panties into his pocket.

The sound of a zipper had her peering down to see Lark unleashing his straining erection from his pants. Seeing his cock coaxed out another shiver of anticipation. He stepped closer, nudging his thickness between her thighs. Then, with his cock in his hand, he stroked the head through her folds. The kiss of his cock's head over her pussy made her writhe against that padded panel.

Her juices slicked him, making that glide all the more intoxicating.

He continued to drag just the head of his dick over her, teasing her far more than his tongue on her clit. When he settled at her opening, she clutched him and forced him closer, to get him to sink into her fully, but he slapped a hand to the padded panel, stopping her attempt. The tease wore on as he dipped in and out, burying just the head into her before withdrawing again.

"Lark. More, please, more."

He obliged by granting her another inch, but he didn't give her the length that she craved. Instead, he kept up his dip and retreat game, but he did give her a bit more of himself every time. Finally, when he sank inside her, he did it fully, sinking entirely. And he didn't stop.

His hand grasped the backs of her knees, and he lifted her off her feet. She locked around him instantly. He pinned his right knee into the panel beneath her. Then, mid-stroke, he rapped his knuckles on the metal between panels.

A whirring sounded as the ride started.

Her eyes widened.

Lark's movements increased.

She knew it was a distraction, which worked. Music blaring from the speakers also distracted her from the ride's noises. Nothing could prevent her from feeling the forces shoving against her, though, flattening her to the panel. That pressure increased, and the anxiety she'd felt the first time she went on the ride returned, even with Lark plunging inside her.

The fact he could still do that was shocking. People usually struggled to push themselves up the panels once the ride was at full speed, but here Lark was holding himself up over her and still pumping his hips. His strength was outstanding. He managed to angle his hips in a way that his cock grazed against her clit, and a cry tore free.

Suddenly, he was dragging her up the panel. Halfway up the wall, he pumped into her, clearly on a mission to grant her pleasure on a ride that usually terrified her. Being shoved against the panel by the g's robbed her of the ability to do anything but take what he could give her. Being forced to surrender like that did something that had her pleasure magnifying.

Her cries got lost in the loud rock music that filled the space.

She clutched him and gave herself over to the ride and to Lark. Eyes closed, she sank. Like a lead weight. She sank into pleasure, into acceptance, into the loss of control that would normally terrify her, but this time gave her a sense of freedom.

She was crying out with the sensations crashing over her when she realized he was tugging her body sideways along the wall. And he didn't stop. He maneuvered her until they were upside down. Hair flowing toward the floor, blood rushing to her head, he pumped into her with an intensity that made her entire body quake around him.

When her orgasm came, her body tensed. She wept as the heat and tingles blasted through her body from core to toes to crown. As she came, her muscles clenched around Lark's cock. Her internal vise on him encouraged him to come. Upside down, his cum drilled her cervix and flooded her. That sensation of being filled startled her with a second orgasm.

Still inside her, Lark carried her degree by degree back to right-side up. And they just held onto each other as the ride pressed them together. Gradually, the ride slowed and then stilled. She untied her legs from around Lark, but she couldn't do more than that. Her heart was racing, and her body was shaking.

Lark pulled out of her slowly. He fixed his pants and extracted her rumpled panties from his pocket. On his knees again, he assisted her with putting her underwear back on. Her legs trembled so much that she laid a hand on his shoulder to steady herself. He noticed. His hands caressed her thighs, massaging the muscles that shivered until they calmed.

"I'm okay," she whispered.

He placed a kiss on both of her thighs before getting up and fetching her jeans from Skull Mask. Once more, he helped her into them. His care stole her breath and filled her with warmth. She'd never had anyone nurture her after an orgasm. Or…ever.

Holding her hand, he directed her toward the exit.

When she passed Skull Mask, he gave her a wink.

Her face burned. Although his back had been to them and the music had drowned out her cries, he'd still heard her earlier moans, and what she and Lark did was quite obvious.

Lark led her to a picnic table outside.

She lowered onto the wooden bench.

Lark nudged his head at a corn dog stand where an employee already stood.

She nodded.

He acquired a pair of corn dogs with a wavy line of mustard on the golden breading, and they ate their corn dogs silently.

When she finished, she set the popsicle stick on a napkin and smiled at Lark. "That was…amazing. And I'm not talking about the corn dog, although that was good, too. But…in there…" She peered at the zero-gravity ride. "…that was…I was genuinely terrified of that ride."

He tilted his head as if asking her for more.

"When I first went on that ride, I was maybe ten, and it gave me so much anxiety. I didn't enjoy it in the least. That's why I didn't go on it with my friends the other night. But with you, just now, that was an experience. I can't believe you moved us like that. That takes insane strength."

He lifted a shoulder.

"Is there a ride you don't like?"

He shook his head.

"What's your favorite ride?"

Another shrug.

She lowered her gaze to the popsicle stick. Wearing the mask while on park grounds was one thing, but why couldn't he talk to her? No one was close enough to hear, and the other guys had cheered while wearing the masks, so a no-talking rule during the off-hours didn't exist, so she didn't understand why he relied on shrugs and nods. She held back the sigh that wanted to escape and picked up her phone to see the time. Thirty minutes had passed since she'd arrived. She had plenty of time to spend with him, but the sadness weighing on her now made her want to leave. So, she chose to do just that.

Flee.

"Um. I'm sorry. I have to go. I forgot I volunteered to clean up the grounds at the haunted house. Lines of people can sure leave a mess." She waved a hand. "Of course you know that."

When she stood, he shoved to his feet. She sensed if he could, he'd grab her, stop her, so she put distance between them. "I'll text you later, okay?"

He nodded.

"Bye." She spun away and left as quickly as she could without making it seem as though she was desperate to get away.

Near the ticket booths at the beginning of the park, she spotted Skull Mask. A glance over her shoulder revealed Lark wasn't following her, so she hustled over. "Hey, you're the guy who called me *baby girl* in the haunted house, right?"

"That was me." His voice was deep.

"And who had fun with my best friend Trina?"

Even though she couldn't see his face, she could hear his grin in his voice. "I definitely remember Trina."

"You caught Lark going down on me."

"Oh, yeah, that was me."

"And you were the one just now operating the zero-gravity ride?"

"The name's Cal."

"Cal...and you're friends with Lark?"

"That's right. I've known him for five years."

"Good, so then you can tell me what's up with him."

Cal hooked his thumbs in the belt loop of his pants. "What do you mean?"

"Why won't he talk to me?"

Cal exhaled. "Shit. You shouldn't be asking me that."

"Why not?"

"It's not for me to tell."

"What's not?" Frustration settled in. "What is he not telling me?"

Cal shook his head.

"Fine. Then you can tell him that until he lets me in on the big secret, today"—she pointed toward the park—"was the last time he'll see me." She attempted to leave, but Cal caught her arm.

"Stop. Don't do that." He raked a hand over his head. "Fuck. He's not going to like that I've told you, but he can't lose you. I can tell he likes you a lot. You're different, and he's damn-near glowing. If you left him…" He shook his head. "I'll tell you. I shouldn't, but I will." He glanced over his shoulder.

They were alone.

Cal turned back. "Lark hasn't spoken a word to you because he can't."

She frowned. "What do you mean?"

Cal sighed. "He has vocal cord paralysis. It happened when he was in a car accident. He was like eighteen. He can't talk."

Her mouth parted. Sadness punched her in the gut. Now it all made sense. Why he wouldn't talk on the phone. Why he conversed in shrugs and nods.

"But he's whispered to me and…I've heard him come."

"From my understanding, he can whisper sometimes, but he uses sign language. I've learned to read it over the years, and the boss knows sign language. But as for everything else, yeah, he could moan for you, but I think it hurts him."

She closed her eyes. That explained him rubbing his throat.

"That's not your fault."

But she still felt at fault. She opened her eyes. "Thanks for telling me."

He bent his neck. "Do you still want me to tell him that he's not going to see you again?"

"No. Don't say anything."

"So, you'll be back?"

"I'll be back."

"Hearing you say that is far sexier than Arnold saying that."

She snorted. "Bye, Cal."

"Wait." He slipped his hands into his pocket. "So…Trina, is she seeing anyone?"

"Nope." Sutton smirked. "Maybe you should visit Haunted House of Raunch in your mask. She'll love that."

"Haunted House of…?"

She showed him their ad on her phone. "Trina plays a banshee. Think Phoebe on *Charmed* when she transforms into a banshee with the white wig and big boobs."

"Damn, I'd love to fuck that."

Sutton laughed. "I bet. Look, I'm going to go. Don't tell Lark anything. I'll talk to him later."

"Alright."

She started to her car.

"Drive safely, baby girl."

She laughed. "You need to stop that."

"Not going to happen."

Cal had made her smile, but in her car, the weight of what Cal had revealed dropped onto her shoulders. She opened an app on her phone and searched for a sign language class she could attend. A local library had a weekly class that she signed up for. If she could do anything, she'd do that so one day they could carry on a conversation and tell each other everything they've ever wanted to say.

9

Pumpkin Daddy

omething was wrong. When he couldn't answer her questions, she'd shut down. And then she left. God, he was making a mistake. If she never came back because she didn't understand, it'd be all his fault. He needed to explain that he couldn't speak in the way she might want him to. And he needed to stop relying on his fucking mask. He ripped it off his head and threw it onto the ground. This damn mask that allowed him to hide even while face to face. Why the hell would he want that with Sutton? Why would he want to hide when she'd shared herself so fully? Why the fuck couldn't he return the favor?

He opened a text chat he hadn't visited in over a year and sent a message to his speech therapist.

> **Lark:** I'm ready to begin again.

> **Lori:** It's good to hear from you again, Lark. Tomorrow noon. I'll skip my lunch to see you.

For her to skip lunch in order to see him as soon as possible told him that she knew how extreme it was that he was asking for help.

> **Lark:** Thank you. I'll be there.

****

Lark sat in Lori's office. While waiting for his appointment, he typed out a text to Sutton.

> **Lark:** Hey, angel. You left fast yesterday. I know you said you had to, but is everything okay?

Debating over whether or not he should send that text, he drummed his fingers against the back of his phone. *Don't be a coward.* He tapped the little paper airplane icon to send the text. Then he held his breath.

The three little dots appeared.

> **Sutton:** Everything is fine.

Fine. When women used the word 'fine,' things were usually not fine at all.

> **Lark:** Are you sure?

> **Sutton:** Yeah.

An incrcdiblc amount of distance lay between them in her replies. She was so far away. His chest tightened.

> **Lark:** Did I do something wrong?

Maybe if she said something about it now, how he didn't talk, perhaps he'd have the courage to text her the truth.

> **Sutton:** No.

That *no* screamed *yes*. It wasn't something he did. It was something he didn't do—talk.

Would she be like the other women who left him

because he was a burden? Because they didn't want to learn ASL? Because being in a relationship with someone mostly mute was too complicated? He'd thought she was different, but he hadn't given her a chance to prove him right. If he lost her now, it wouldn't be because he couldn't talk. It'd be because he hadn't been honest.

Before he could respond, she texted back.

> **Sutton:** Yesterday was amazing. I had a breakthrough on that ride, and probably not in any way a therapist would suggest.

She added laughing-crying emoji.

He smirked at that.

> **Lark:** I doubt they would've told you to 'get off' on the ride.

> **Sutton:** Oh, but how effective.

She was joking. That was a positive sign.

The office door opened, and a patient stepped out.

Lori stood there in black slacks and a white blouse. "Lark?"

He tapped out a text to Sutton.

Lark: I won't be able to text for the next hour, but don't go anywhere.

Sutton: I'm not leaving.

His chest expanded with those words.

He entered Lori's office.

"Hi, Lark," she said and signed. "It's been a long time. Have a seat."

He lowered onto a high-backed chair.

"I was surprised to get that text from you yesterday. What brings you in today?"

"I met someone," he signed back and mouthed.

Lori smiled.

"It's new, and she's perfect, and I'm screwing it up already. I don't want to screw it up."

Her brows bunched. "How are you doing that?"

Lark grimaced. "Because she doesn't know I can't speak."

Now Lori full-on frowned. "How'd you manage to start a relationship and not reveal that part about yourself?"

"It's a long story. I want to do the right thing, but it's hard for me to let people in."

Lori nodded.

"I want to let her in, but to do that I need to work on myself. That's why I'm here." He breathed deeply.

"I'm ready to accept help."

Her smile returned. "I'm proud of you."

"Don't be proud of me yet. Be proud if I return."

She eyed him.

"I'm kidding. I'll come back."

"Good. We'll start with a few tongue exercises."

"My tongue's mobility is fine. Trust me. No complaints there."

She rolled her eyes. "I haven't seen you in a year. You probably haven't spoken much during that time. Extracurricular tongue activities don't count. We need to establish a base line. First up, tongue exercises."

So, they did all the silly tongue exercises—sticking it out, moving it from side to side, touching it to each tooth in his mouth. After that, he blew bubbles and sucked on a straw. He definitely didn't have any problems with sucking, either.

"Okay," Lori said. "Now we'll awaken your vocal cords with lip and tongue trills."

That wasn't difficult. He didn't have any problems with breath control.

"Good. We'll move on to vocal function exercises."

And this was the part that sucked. The yawn-sigh warm-up was the easiest part, but sustaining sounds was hard when he couldn't get his damn vocal cords to go above a whisper.

Lori didn't force him to go above that whisper, though.

"Even in a whisper, we can train your vocal cords to hit the high, clear sounds and the low, resonant sounds."

He nodded, but his frustration was already building.

"You're doing great, Lark. This is your first day back at this, and you're excelling."

Her encouragement ushered tears to his eyes.

She handed him a tissue.

He gripped it in his hands and bent forward. With his elbows on his knees, he fisted his hands to his forehead. Tears zipped down his cheeks.

"I know it's hard, Lark," she said. "And it's okay to be frustrated."

He nodded against his fists. Then he lowered his hands to sign, "I just want to talk to her."

"And one day, you will. In your way. What's her name?"

"Sutton."

"Well, that's an easy one. Do you want to practice it?"

"I've been practicing it on my own."

She nodded for him to continue.

He inhaled and exhaled slowly before making the first attempt. "Ssss...ught...tonnn." He felt the harshness of the "ught" in his vocal cord, so Lori had him repeat it. Then he created the "n" sound again and again. When he finally said Sutton's name in a deeper pitch than he'd been able to speak in over a year, his eyes widened in shock.

Lori laughed. "Well done, Lark. Now, you know the drill. Rest your vocal cords. Hot teas, alternate cold and warm compresses, over-the-counter pain reliever as needed. Continue the warm-up exercises at home, but don't push it. I'll get you on my schedule for once a week. When your vocal cords are stronger, we'll increase it to two times a week. Sound good?"

"Yes."

"It was nice to see you again."

"You, too. Thank you," he signed and mouthed.

"You're welcome. Now no more talking for the rest of the day."

"Yes, ma'am."

After speech therapy he stopped at Books & Brews for one of Benny's magical teas. As soon as he stepped up to the counter, she frowned. "You look miserable," she signed.

He nodded, but tomorrow he'd be worse.

"One large tea coming right up."

"Thank you." He glanced around the space. No Sutton. He waved his hand to get Benny's attention. "I have a question. Yesterday when I came in, a woman came up to the counter after me. She has a scar." And he traced the scar along his neck.

"Yes, Sutton. Why?"

"She's the one I've been seeing."

For a split second, Benny's face lit up. But a frown quickly replaced her smile. "Wait. What? No. Hold on. Let me finish your tea." She made his tea, capped it, and handed it over. Then she said to her co-worker, "I need to take five." She didn't wait for her co-worker's response and dragged Lark over to a private corner. When she signed, her hands were fast. "But the two of you sat at different tables. You didn't acknowledge each other. And, yes, I was watching because I was thinking about how cute the two of you would be together. I noticed you looking at her. Except you said you were getting laid so I…" She blinked. "You and Sutton are banging each other?"

"Yes."

"But…" She shook her head. "But you acted like you don't know each other."

"That's because she hasn't seen me without my mask."

Benny blinked. "You've been banging her with a mask on?"

"Yes."

"One, that's hot. Two, that's a bit crazy. How many times have you two…?"

"Three separate occasions."

She gaped. "And Sutton still doesn't know what you look like?"

He lifted a shoulder.

"Then I'm guessing she doesn't know about your speech difficulties?"

He shook his head.

She smacked the back of his head. "You idiot."

He explained that he'd just come back from speech therapy for the first time in a year and it was all because of Sutton. She was his driving force. His motivation. His inspiration.

His angel.

Benny laid her hands to her chest. "Tell her that. Text it. Write it. Just let her know."

"I will. Soon. I promise." He just had to get up the courage to do it.

He practiced his exercises every day and texted Sutton. She didn't feel as distant in her texts anymore, but a space remained between them that he didn't want to be there. He yearned to see her again. She texted him that she started attending a class. The teacher had offered her daily one-on-one tutoring for an affordable price that Sutton had been going to. He didn't know what she was taking a class for, and he didn't want to press if she didn't want to say. He didn't even know what her day job was other than doing administrative work.

God, he was lame. By trying to keep his secret, he'd inadvertently built a wall between them. He needed to knock that fucking wall down.

****

Friday night, he did his thing. He stalked girls who giggled and squealed. He sized up the men with them, as if challenging them. It was all a part of his role. Be the mouth-watering bad boy that could steal your girl with nothing but a look through the eyeholes of a mask. That was how they all won the girls there. He enjoyed it. He wouldn't lie. The men trying to look and act tough never failed to amuse him. He had fun mocking them with his height and silence that claimed he was deadly.

When the men flexed their muscles in a show meant to make him back down, he flexed back, making it clear he would do anything to have their girl. Even if he had no interest what-so-ever in the woman in question. But the women who were clearly intrigued by his attention invigorated his blood in a way that the anger of their partners didn't. Arousal pumped through him just by the willingness in their eyes. That arousal was what gave him his edge, making the men sense a threat and the women questioning if they would ditch their man for one night's fun with a masked stranger.

While he was turned on by the reactions, he wasn't interested in anyone. Not anymore. He sat on the barrel next to the alley, his post where he could take a break and stalk passersby with his stare. If any of them seemed like they'd be a fun target, he'd get up, but no one was catching his eye, so he leaned back, eyes closed, and breathed in the night air. Like this, he created even more of a stir, like a sleeping dragon. He let them believe he could spring up and come at them in any second, but he didn't intend to do that. This was a moment for himself.

A slight chill had fallen over Florida, unlike the night he'd met Sutton when it had been stifling. A cool breeze caressed his chest. He drew in another deep breath. Giggles drifted toward him, but he ignored them.

"You wanna be my pumpkin daddy?"

Laughter followed the woman's catcall.

He arched a brow beneath his mask and decided not to take the bait.

A beat of silence after they passed by, and then, "Boo."

He shot to his feet and whirled around.

Sutton stood there, having used the alley to sneak up on him.

He lifted his mask over his mouth and snatched her up. Kissing her with a savage hunger. She latched onto him and allowed him to lead her into the shadows where no one could see them. He pressed her against the wall to devour her lips more thoroughly.

"I can't…I can't…"

He didn't like those words coming out of her mouth, so he didn't stop kissing her, hoping to erase them from her lips, but she inched him back.

"I can't stay long. I just…" She was breathless. "I just got off work. I have to go to Haunted House of Raunch. I can't stay long, but I needed to see you."

He settled his face at the crook of her neck and planted gentle kisses along her scar. *I'm so glad you came here, angel. I was afraid I'd never see you again.*

She sighed. "Lark. Wait. I need to say…" She took a shaky breath. Her hands slid from his head and formed gently around the sides of his neck. "I know."

He tilted his head, not understanding.

"I know," she repeated. "Cal told me."

Son-of-a-bitch.

"I get it," she whispered. "I understand now. I don't care if you can't talk to me. I really don't. It's okay. It's okay because…" She bit her bottom lip. Then she let go of his neck and signed while saying, "I'm learning for you."

Seeing her hands signing that was a beautiful sight.

His breath left him.

No one had ever done anything like that before, aside from family. Cal didn't even know how to sign but at least understood some ASL after seeing Lark signing for so long. Unlike the women he'd been in a relationship with who hadn't bothered. They hadn't cared. They let his limitations define him, and they treated his struggle as a reason their relationship wouldn't work, so then it didn't.

Sutton was learning ASL.

His breathing quickened.

"The class I've been going to..." She signed slowly. "It's an ASL class. I've been going all week."

He couldn't contain his emotions anymore and crushed his mouth to hers. His emotions were so strong that his erection was swift. He pumped his hips, grinding his cock through his pants, between her legs, against her clothed pussy.

She moaned into his mouth.

That moan had Lark snapping.

He whipped her around and lowered her onto all fours. Then he was tugging her jeans and panties to mid-thigh. Her bare ass was so damn gorgeous. He yanked open his own pants to unleash himself. His hand fisted around his cock while his other hand caressed her ass. God, he could come like this. Seeing her ass, fondling it, he could come all over her beautiful, round cheeks. Instead, he slid his cock into the crack between her thighs and rubbed it over her pussy. She was so amazingly wet that he couldn't stop from growling.

"Don't hurt your throat," she panted.

Her concern made him want her more.

He thrust inside her, smooth and clean.

She moaned.

Overcome with the need to feel her pussy milk his cock of everything he had in him, he plowed into her. His cock sank into her wet, dripping pussy with squelching sounds that drove him wild. He rocked faster into her, hungry for her to shatter on his dick.

Her moans mixed with the sounds of their bodies mating.

People walked past the alley laughing and giddy with excitement. Their proximity to those people, the thrill of someone noticing him taking Sutton in an animalistic frenzy had him taking her even harder.

He grabbed a handful of her hair and carefully wrenched her head back so she'd look at the entrance to the alley and all the people walking past. So close. Feet away from hearing her moans. Feet away from stumbling upon them. When Cal had walked in on Lark eating out her pretty pussy, she'd almost allowed Cal to stand there and watch Lark make her come on his tongue. She'd been turned on by that, and now, peering at the street full of people filtering by, she rocked back against him. Faster and faster. Her moans morphed into cries.

Grasping her hips, tugging her backward as he plunged forward, she wailed. *Fuck, yes, let them all hear you. Let them know how good I can fuck this sweet pussy. Let them all know you want me to fill you with my cum. Let them all fucking know it, angel. Come for me right now*. He thrust with each word he thought next. *Come. Right. Fucking. Now*.

And she did.

He sank into her, drawing out her orgasm as her cunt palpitated around him. She cried out while still rocking back. Her muscles squeezed cum out of him. He plowed through his orgasm as more and more cum spurted forth. When the last of it left him, his movements finally shuddered to a halt, and he bent over her, panting and spent.

Beneath him, she quivered from her own orgasm.

He withdrew slowly and sat back on his heels. His

body was still shaking from his release as he tucked his depleted cock into his pants and rezipped.

She pulled up her underwear and pants, faced him, and crawled close. Her hands embraced his face. "Did you hurt your throat?"

He skimmed his fingertips down her cheeks. Rather than answer, because he definitely had, he kissed her softly, a direct contrast to how he'd taken her a moment ago. Their kiss was so achingly sweet that his chest vibrated with the love he couldn't say, but so badly wanted her to know he harbored.

She whimpered.

He kissed her through her whimpers until she broke contact.

Forehead to forehead, she said, "I don't want to leave, but I have to go. I'm going to be late."

He nodded. Then he signed for the first time to her. "It's okay. Go, angel."

Her brows lowered slightly. "I know you told me it's okay to go, but that last one...I'm not sure what that meant."

He removed his cell phone from his pocket, opened a note app, and typed: *Angel.* Then he showed her the screen.

Her lips lifted into a smile. "Angel."

He laid a hand to her cheek before signing. "You are my angel."

She touched her lips to his and spoke as their mouths still touched. "We'll text later?"

He nodded.

She waved before getting up and hurrying away.

He stayed on his knees because in that position he

could thank the universe for what had happened right there. Sutton had accepted him, and he had fallen in love with her with every fiber of his being.

10

The Dead Bride's Bed

Sutton arrived home late after the haunted house closed. In her bathroom, she used a pile of baby wipes to remove her joker makeup. Then she lathered up in her shower and scrubbed away Lark and the remnants of makeup. Exhausted from acting for hours, she crawled into bed with her phone. Tired though she was, she video called Lark.

Except, the call didn't go through.

Frowning, she laid her phone on her nightstand and hugged her pillow to her head. They'd made strives today, but he still didn't want her to see his face?

Why?

She hadn't asked Cal about the mask, because she didn't think it was the issue, but maybe the mask was a part of it. Perhaps not talking and Lark's mask went hand-in-hand. Not talking could be a symptom for why he wore the mask and didn't want her to see his face, but the why eluded her. Sleep was hard for her to catch, and when she did sleep, it was fleeting.

In the morning, a text from Lark waited.

> **Lark:** I'm sorry for not answering your video call last night. That orgasm took it out of me. I drove straight home and flopped onto my bed. I was out instantly.

Well, a night of worrying for nothing. He hadn't been hiding. He had been a man utterly satisfied and spent. That thought made her smile.

> **Sutton:** I'm glad I could help you to sleep like a baby. How are you feeling this morning?

> **Lark:** Well fucked and well rested.

She laughed.

> **Sutton:** And your throat?

> **Lark:** It's okay, angel.

She frowned, sensing that he was holding back.

> **Sutton:** The truth, Lark. Please. You don't have to keep anything

> **Lark:** It's sore, but that's to be expected. I resumed speech therapy earlier in the week. It hurts, but my crappy vocal cords will get stronger. One day, I'll say a full sentence to you. That's another promise. And I don't break promises.

Tears ballooned in her eyes.
She didn't know what to say to that.

> **Lark:** You still there?

Her fingers shook as she typed.

> **Sutton:** I'm here. I'm not leaving you, Lark. I just didn't know what to say to that.

what to say to that.

> **Lark:** You don't have to say anything. What you've already told me is enough. Have a good day, angel.

> **Sutton:** You, too.

Before work, she stopped in at Books & Brews for her dirty chai latte. On her way in, someone was leaving, and she nearly ran right into him.

"Oh my gosh, I'm so sorry." She peered up at a man with dark blond hair and chestnut brown eyes. Locks of his hair had fallen across his forehead. He appeared startled, and she supposed running pointblank into someone and almost splashing what was likely a scalding drink down his front warranted a startled look. "That could've been disastrous," she said. "You're good?"

He nodded and offered her a kind smile.

"Sorry again." She stepped aside to let him leave. On her way to the counter, she caught Benny smacking her forehead and shaking her head.

"Something wrong?"

"Nothing. I'm just surrounded by idiots. That's all."

Her co-worker shot her a look.

"Not you," Benny said and shifted back to Sutton.

"Your usual?"

"Please. And a pumpkin raisin muffin."

"Comin' right up."

As Benny fixed her drink, she slid a look over at Sutton.

"What?"

"You're positively glowing this morning."

Sutton glanced around and leaned over the counter. "I had the most incredible sex last night. It was…" She licked her lips, creating a smacking sound. "Carnal and frenzied and holy shit I want more."

"Damn, girl. *I* want that." She grinned at Sutton. "Good for you."

Sutton sighed with every ounce of satisfaction in her body. "For the first time, I feel like I can be myself with him. I've never had that before. He accepts all my scars. The visible ones and the hidden ones."

"You deserve that, and I'm so happy you've found it."

"So am I."

Benny handed her a cup of frothy chai tea with a shot of espresso and a plate with a spice-fragrant, orange-colored muffin speckled with plump raisins.

"Thank you."

"Enjoy."

Sutton sat at a free table and sipped a bit of froth and espresso-strengthened chai. The first hit made her sigh. Her eyelids lowered, and she enjoyed another long sip. Mornings were always made better after she had her dirty chai latte.

Ding.

She picked up her cell phone.

A text from Lark waited.

> **Lark:** Will an angel visit me tonight?

She nibbled on her bottom lip.

> **Sutton:** You might be blessed with a visit, but I can't say she'll be an angel.

> **Lark:** Angels with horns are the best kind. Let me see those horns.

She laughed under her breath.

> **Sutton:** If she shows up, will you corrupt her more? You might get her to do some naughty, nasty things.

> **Lark:** Oh, she already has.

Her teeth clamped onto her lip.

> **Lark:** The way she had me coming in her throat when we met, that was naughty. The way she thrust back against me while I fucked her in public, that was nasty.

She clamped her thighs together.

> **Lark:** Tonight, if my angel visits me, there's no telling just how naughty or nasty we will get. We might make angelic choirs weep and demon hordes cheer.

Her face heated.

> **Sutton:** Sounds like a plan.

> **Lark:** Tonight, angel.

Her heart raced with the promises tonight would bring, so all she could text in response was one word: *Tonight.*

All day, she considered what they'd do once together.

All day, she was incredibly horny.

After getting home from her admin job, she scarfed down a peanut butter and jelly sandwich before driving to the haunted house. In the women's bathroom for employees, she used the spread of makeup to paint on her joker's face. Creating her character's face was second nature now. In the beginning, it had taken her an hour to complete the look exactly how she wanted it. Now, her hand was sure, quick, and she was staring at her own version of a mask.

She smiled, stretching that joker grin to insane lengths. The idea of visiting Lark at All Horrors' Eve like this, in her full joker makeup and attire, filled her with excitement. She fixed her orange and black wig into place. Lark had enjoyed her costume and act when he'd visited her at Haunted House of Raunch, so she figured he'd blow his mind seeing her like this on his turf.

For the next hour, her anticipation grew. The more she creeped out guests, and probably aroused most of them, the more she squirmed from the lust building inside her. Jesus, she needed a release fast.

During a lull between groups of guests, Trina visited Sutton. Trina cocked her head to the side. "You look like you're going to burst out of your skin. What's going on?"

Sutton danced in place from the desire surging through her, but that only made her loins hungrier. "I'm super horny. I'm waiting for the night to end so I can rush over to Lark and fuck his brains out. Or let him fuck my brains out. I haven't decided yet. As it is, we'll probably fuck each other's brains out at the same time."

"Girl, then what the hell are you still doing here? Go get railed."

"I can't leave."

"Yes, you can. We have extras just for this."

"We do *not* have extras so I can run off to have sex at a Halloween theme park."

"I don't know what better of a reason to have extras than for this reason. Hell, I left last night so I could get fucked every which way by Skull Mask."

Sutton blinked. "You did?" She pointed a finger up and down to indicate Trina's costume. "Like that?"

"Hell yeah. I thought I would surprise him, that he wouldn't even know it was me from that night, but *someone* told him that I portray a slutty banshee."

Sutton grimaced. "Sorry."

"Don't be. He was hard the instant he saw me. He dragged me into the haunted house and fucked me on the floor in the graveyard. The fog covered us, and our moans mixed with the howls from the speakers, but his masked buddies were there, surrounding us, jerking off while watching us, and it was the hottest thing I've ever experienced."

Sutton crossed her legs. "Oh, God, please stop. I really am so horny that one word, one visual, one movement could have me coming."

Trina smirked. "Then go and let Lark take care of you."

She usually wouldn't bail, but she was desperate. "Fine. This once." She turned to go and Trina smacked her ass. The vibration of the teasing slap shot right to her pussy, and she moaned. "God, don't do that."

Trina's laughter followed her as she ran out of there. Driving to the theme park, she was definitely over the speed limit, and she was fully prepared to tell any cop who pulled her over that she was deeply sorry for speeding, but she did it because she was on the verge of coming all over her leather seat.

Saturday night, a week before Halloween, the parking lot was packed. She had to park far from the entrance. The trek to the ticket booth only increased her yearnings.

"Hi." Her body vibrated with needs. "You probably don't recognize me. I'm Sutton. I'm Lark's—"

"I know who you are. You can go right in."

"Thank you."

She made her way through the crowds on the lookout for Lark. When she spotted the pumpkin mask, she slowed. The bat rested against his shoulder, and he was trailing behind two young women who were holding onto each other and peering back at him. She stopped near the haunted house to watch him do his thing.

He swooped his bat in a circle, slicing it past the girl on the left.

She let out a squeal.

Then he did the same to the girl on the right.

She yelped.

They huddled together.

Lark stepped closer and bore down on them.

From her place, leaning against the wall, she jittered with excitement. They could probably smell him. The leather of his vest. The rubber of the mask. The musk of his cologne. The sweetness of his sweat. He smelled like sex on Halloween night, and that was something that could arouse her any time she caught a whiff.

They could probably feel his body heat, too. Hear

his breathing.

She wanted his body heat to surround her. She wanted to hear his breathing in her ears as he slipped inside her. Jealousy seared through her veins. The urge to drag him away from them was fierce, but this was a job. It was a game. Pretend.

With her, it wasn't a game or pretend. It had never been.

His head tilted toward her, and he jolted to a stop.

She did her little sway and chaotic head jerk from side to side to tell him that he wasn't seeing things. She was real.

The girls continued on.

Lark was rooted to the spot.

Suddenly, he was running. Halfway across the street, he dropped down and slid across the pavement on knee pads and gloved hands. Sparks shot into the air. A couple of feet away, he popped to his feet, and then he was looming over her.

She gaped. "Holy shit, that was hot."

He expelled air from his nose, indicating at amused laughter.

She gripped the sides of his ripped vest and tugged him down so her breath ghosted across the mouth of his pumpkin mask. "Give me ten seconds, and then come find me."

She tore free and entered the haunted house. In her head, she counted down. The skull masks let her pass. She dodged the outstretched hands, shot down the hall where she'd hidden before, and slithered around the table in the bloody laboratory.

The first night, after Lark had left, she'd finished

the rest of the haunted house, so she knew exactly where she was going, where she wanted him to fuck her. After the blood-splattered room was a tiny space with two-way mirrors on both sides. Those fake mirrors were marred with deep cracks, and on the other side, spooky women with large eyes, wild hair, and blood streaming down to their elbows pounded on the mirrors as if trying to break through them.

Past that, zombies lurched. She darted past them and entered a hall, which was another break between attractions to give the next scare actors a moment to get into place. The room beyond this hallway was her final destination. She flung back the ripped lace and peered around.

The bed she recalled was there, draped in black. The rest of the space was decked out like a gothic bedroom. When she'd walked through this part last time, a dead bride in a stained white gown had haunted this space. That scare actor wasn't there now, giving Sutton the opportunity to crawl onto the bed after stripping out of her panties. In the middle of it, she propped herself up on her elbows and opened her legs, so when Lark came into the bride's bedroom and found her, he got an eyeful. For fun, she'd been researching how to sign curse words, as one would do, of course, and she used that knowledge to sign an order.

"Come here and fuck me good."

Yanking down his zipper, Lark came toward her. He gripped his cock with one hand, flattened her to the mattress with the other, and dove inside her in one fluid motion aided by just how wet she was. His cock stretching her stole her breath. She arched her back from the sheer pleasure that rippled through her.

He didn't give her a chance to do more than that before he pounded into her, causing the bed's scratched-up headboard to rap against the wall.

She couldn't contain the cries that broke loose. His frantic needs consumed her as he pumped his hips, filling her with his cock stroke for stroke. She rammed her hips into his, eager to match his veracity. Her orgasm was gearing up to shatter her into a glorious mess all over Lark and that bed when the scare actor in a wedding dress ran into the room.

"What the hell is wrong with the two of you?" she hissed.

Lark slowed, but he didn't stop entirely.

Still, the dramatic change in pace had her orgasm vanishing.

"Will you stop that!" The bride threw a small, black decorative pillow at Lark. It whacked him in the back before bouncing off him to the floor. "A group of teens are coming." She snatched up a blanket that had fallen from the force of their throes and tossed it over them, casting them into darkness. "Don't move, and don't make a sound."

Lark stilled. His hands tightened around her waist.

The sounds of a group of people approaching had her stamping her lips together. Her body screamed to keep on going, to do whatever she needed to in order to reach her climax. She gritted her teeth and clamped her thighs around Lark as if she were an anaconda. With the way her body raged inside, like a sea caught in a category five hurricane, she needed an anchor, and Lark was that—her anchor.

The bride began her show. Sutton didn't know how long it'd take to get through, but it better be quick because Lark was shivering.

Shit. He was struggling, too. To go from fucking her with abandon to suddenly having to stop without crossing the finish line, his body had to feel as though it was about to crack. She couldn't see him. All she could do was touch him. With careful movements, she shifted her hands from his shoulders to his face and peeled the mask above his nose. Then she brought her lips to his. The kiss was soft, with the goal of soothing him, and he kissed her back just as tenderly.

In their little cocoon, Lark's body heat swooped around her. His breathing filled her ears when their lips disconnected but remained touching. The kiss hadn't been enough to calm either of them. Her body was begging, pleading, damn-near ready to start sobbing to finish what they'd started. She performed Kegels with him buried inside her. God, it felt so good to squeeze him with her internal muscles. She'd orgasmed before from doing Kegels when she was horny. Without a doubt in her mind, she'd come. Especially with Lark filling her.

Lark's fingertips dug into her waist. A small groan rumbled in his throat.

That sound hinted at his struggle to maintain composure, and it was sexy as hell. She yearned for him to come inside her. With a group of people at the foot of the bed, she desired that release that she'd been denied. Unable to hold back any longer, she rolled her hips slowly.

Lark shifted his hands to her hips. Instead of

stilling her, he gripped her. He appeared to be holding on for dear life as she maintained the motion of her hips.

"Something's moving under the blanket."

"It's whatever killed the bride."

"Freddie!"

The scare actor let out a shriek, and several screams filled the air.

Feet pounded against the floor.

Lark's body shuddered.

His control snapped, and he resumed sinking into her.

She couldn't swallow her moans.

"The coast is clear, you sick pervs," the scare actor spat. "You have five minutes to fuck and leave."

Footsteps departed.

Lark swept the blanket off them and took Sutton with new gusto.

She could see his mouth in the dim lighting, and damn. Yanking him down, she crushed her mouth to his. A gasp escaped her when he switched their positions with ease. His hands on her hips yanked her forward, and she got the hint. Rising up over him, she rode him. Her hips were like a whip in her determination to get them to break in the next sixty seconds. She arched her back, braced her hands on his thighs, and attacked his cock with her pussy. Cries peeled from her one after the other.

She hunched over him and met his stare through the eyeholes of his mask. "Lark…"

His hips shot off the bed.

His cum pooled inside her.

She came as he did.

Her orgasm rocked her body in waves.

Beneath her, he convulsed as he continued to leak cum.

She bent over him and whispered in his ear, "That's it. Give it all to me."

He groaned, and she cupped a hand to his throat to squeeze it gently, muffling the rest of his moan. His larynx vibrated against her fingertips. When he finished, he held her close. She nuzzled his neck and planted kisses along his throat. With each breath, his chest lifted her up.

"Lark, I—"

"What the hell?!"

Sutton had been about to admit she was in love with him, but the bride stood beside the bed. "The two of you aren't supposed to cuddle." She waved her hands. "Get out of here. Now."

Sutton climbed off Lark. "Sorry."

"Whatever, pervette."

Sutton couldn't stop from laughing. Pervette. Maybe she'd let her alter ego take over too much, but she couldn't get herself to care right then.

11

Ferris Wheel

ark snatched Sutton's hand and led her through the back of the haunted house to the outdoors. The whole way, Sutton was giggling. On the street, he faced her and titled his head.

"She called me pervette. I'm already imagining my costume for next year's haunted house."

He shook his head. Since she didn't know much ASL, he located his phone, opened the note app, and typed: *You're my pervette. No one else's.* He rotated the phone around so she could read his words.

She laughed. "Yes, I am." And she signed that, too.

He tapped another message into the app: *Where'd you learn how to sign 'come here and fuck me good'?*

She grinned. "The Internet."

He snorted and typed: *And where'd you learn how*

121

to hold my throat like that?

"Also the Internet."

Smiling, he wrote another message. *You had asked me what my favorite ride was*. He curled his fingers around her chin and tipped her head back.

When her gaze met his again, her smile was soft. "Can you show me how to sign Ferris wheel?"

He curved his index and middle fingers and rotated his hands in circles.

She mimicked it. "Looks like a bunny is trying to claw you."

He chuckled soundlessly. Well, she wasn't wrong.

Wondering if she'd understand, he signed and mouthed, "Do you want to go for a ride with me?"

"Yes."

They walked up to Dante, the masked operator, who let them onto the old-fashioned two-seater car. As the wheel reversed, Lark wrote out a message to Sutton and showed it to her. *When it's late and no one is in line, they let me on and stop the ride at the very top so I can just sit there and look out at everything. I want to show you how peaceful it is.*

Her eyes sparkled in the lights lining the Ferris wheel. "Thank you."

The ride slowly lifted them higher and higher. At the top, the ride came to a gentle stop that swung their car back and forth.

From way up there, everything looked different—the streets spotted with scare actors and guests, the rides lit up with neon lights, the haunted house and funhouse seemingly calm and quiet. It was a perspective that he liked. After the craziness of the theme park, the silence up in the starry sky helped to regulate him. It calmed him after a long night.

Sutton leaned over the gate in front of them to look at the ground. "It's neat up here." Then she tipped back to admire the stars twinkling above. "It's beautiful."

He cupped her chin with his fingers so he could stare into her eyes. With his right hand, he signed. "You are beautiful."

She shook her head. "I don't look like myself."

He pulled out his phone so he could share every word on his mind. *Like this...painted up and dressed up...you are beautiful. Like yourself...with your black hair down, your scars visible, and that angelic smile on your face...you are beautiful. You are so fucking beautiful, Sutton.*

She swallowed. "Lark..."

He typed furiously. *I need you to know how damn beautiful you are.*

Tears, like liquid diamonds, formed in her eyes.

Have the men before me not made sure you knew that?

She shook her head.

Then they didn't fucking deserve you. I will make sure you know how beautiful you are. I'll prove it to you every day.

She reached for his mask, and he couldn't stop from flinching back. His reaction didn't go unnoticed. She paused before resuming her task and folded the bottom half of his mask above his nose. Laying a hand to his jaw, she laid her lips to his and gave him a kiss that made his heart quiver. Pain existed there from a past he didn't know. But gratitude also seeped through the kiss. She was grateful for his words. Except, he didn't want her to be grateful. He wanted her to believe them, accept them, know them to be the truth. Hoping to get that across, he kissed her with everything he had in him.

She shifted back, breathless. Then she cuddled into his side.

He secured an arm around her and held her close.

They sat high in the sky, gazing out at the park, in each other's arms. This was what Lark wanted every night. Here. With her. Every single night.

"We sure make a pair," she said. "A man in a pumpkin mask and a chaotic joker."

Yes, we do, baby. We're the perfect pair, he thought.

"I have a funny story to tell you that I was reminded of when I started taking ASL lessons. My first day of school for third grade, my teacher told us that if we wanted water to put our hand up while showing a W with our fingers. If we needed to use the bathroom, she showed us how to sign the letter B. And she said that she would have one of two replies. She asked if any of us knew what this meant." Sutton signed *no*. "Trina was sitting across from me. She knew basic sign language and she announced that it meant no. Then our teacher asked what this meant." Sutton signed *yes*. "And I said, 'knock.' I felt so stupid when everyone else said it meant yes." She covered her face with her hands while laughing. "It still embarrasses me."

That was the cutest damn story, and her reaction to the memory was adorable. She had been young. If a teacher made the sign for *yes*, a child could think they were getting permission and being reminded to knock. It was logical.

His mask was still lifted, so he kissed her temple.

Sighing, she snuggled closer.

He closed his eyes to sink into this feeling…and into this moment.

They stayed like that for a while, and Lark loved every second of it.

"You know…" Sutton faced him. "We're really high up. No one can see us."

He tilted his head, wondering what she was getting at. Did she want to do something deliciously naughty up here? Because he wouldn't say no if she did.

"Can you take your mask off for me?"

But he wasn't expecting her to say that.

He lifted his phone to tell her the truth: *I've worn this mask for so long. I don't know what it's like to meet someone new and let them see my face.*

"But surely you don't wear your mask in public."

An invisible mask. I get coffee, gas, and I have groceries delivered. Aside from that, I'm either wearing this mask or hiding behind a screen.

"Why?"

It's easier to hide behind a mask than let everyone see the real me.

"And the real you is?"

A man who lost his voice in more than one way, which made him want to hide, even while face to face.

"Even though I know about your voice, you still want to hide from me?"

I don't want to hide from you, angel.

"But you can't take off your mask?"

He didn't know what to say to that, so he didn't type anything into the note app, and because he didn't do that, Sutton angled her head away. Hating himself and questioning his firm grasp on his need to stay hidden even in plain sight, he stroked his hand down her hair, forgetting she wore a wig until he touched it.

She turned back. "Do you have scars on your face? From your accident? Do you have scars? Because I won't care. You know I have scars. You've seen them. Whatever scars you have, I will love them. I swear."

He shook his head and signed: *No, I don't have scars on my face.*

"Can...?" She exhaled and peered at her hands. "Do you have a selfie I can see? That could be a good first step. It's less direct."

He considered it. Her request to see a picture made sense, so he opened the photo app on his phone and scrolled back, searching for a photo he could show her. No, he didn't take selfies. Most of the photos were of Stella. Smiling beneath his mask, he showed her a photo of the sweetest Golden Retriever.

She laughed. "Okay, who is that?"

He spelled out Stella's name.

"She's adorable, but she's not what I was hoping for."

He rotated the phone back and continued the hunt until he found a photo he'd snapped of him and Amy. In the picture, he faced away from the camera and the sun glared above their heads, slightly distorting the image, but he was visible. Most of him anyway. He knew better than to show her a picture of him with another woman, though. Keeping the screen hidden, he

126

signed: *sister*.

She frowned. "Shoot. I learned that. It's a name or title…"

He showed her his phone, pointed at Amy, and signed 'sister' again.

"Sister. That's your sister?"

He nodded.

She held his phone and stared at the screen for several moments. "Well, you're not cute." Her gaze met his. "You're ridiculously handsome."

He snorted and signed: *Thank you*.

She studied the photo a while longer before relinquishing his phone. "That's all I get? A side profile? I mean, it's a beautiful photo, but…I want more." She searched his mask as if she could see through it. "I want to know the man I've been having incredible sex with us. I want to know *you*, Lark."

"You know me," he signed.

She shook her head. "But I don't. Not really. Not as much as I'd like. I'm getting to know you, but I can't truly know you if you keep secrets, if you keep your face hidden from me."

He sat forward and gripped the rail in front of him. She had no idea how hard she was making this. None. Why was it so hard? She meant everything to him.

Why was this so fucking hard?

"Okay." She laid a hand on his shoulder. "It's okay. I'm sorry. I'll stop." She tugged on his arm gently. "Come here. Relax. Come here."

He sat back.

She angled toward him, lifted her legs onto the chair to tent them over his lap, and wrapped her arms around his middle.

He slung an arm around her shoulders to envelope her in a hug.

They held each other for a long time.

Below, workers shut down rides.

Neon lights flashed off.

"We should probably get down now," she said.

Wishing they had more time up there, he texted Dante. Seconds later, the Ferris wheel jolted, and they began their descent.

On the ground, Sutton laced her fingers with his. "Walk me to my car."

Hand in hand, they walked silently through the park as workers packed up booths and security searched the grounds to make sure all the guests had left.

In the parking lot, Sutton led him to a little red sports car. She pulled a key fob from a zippered pocket in her dress and pressed the button to unlock the car. A beep sounded. At the driver's side door, she faced him.

He was expecting a goodnight kiss. He was not expecting to see tears streaming down her face and distorting her makeup. His heart sank in his chest. One hand to her wet cheek, he lifted the other and signed: *Why are you crying*?

"Because I can't." Her voice cracked.

The emotion in her words was like a fist to the gut. "Can't what?"

She burrowed into him and latched onto him as if he were a life preserver. "I can't."

His thoughts were frantic. *Can't what, baby? What can't you do*?

"I can't do this. Us. I can't…"

He flinched back and cupped her face with his hands. His gaze searched hers. The heartbreak in them shattered him.

"I can't be in a relationship with someone who won't let me see his face."

Cold, stark fear.

"I care so much for you, Lark, but I can't. I'm so sorry. I thought I could, but I just can't." She tore out of his hold, flung open her car door, and dove inside.

He caught the door when she went to slam it.

"Let the door go, Lark. Please. Let *me* go. You need to let me go."

His body felt frigid.

"Please, Lark, let go."

He didn't know what to do, so he released the door.

But she paused in the act of closing it.

Hope filled him.

"Just promise me that you won't stop going to speech therapy. One day, you will find a woman who you'll want to be totally yourself with, who you will remove your mask for, and you will tell her something with your voice. Your real voice, as soft as it may be. A full sentence. Something that will make any other sentence that you could possibly say pale in comparison because that's how powerful it will be. Do that. Okay? Do that."

And just like that…hopeless.

"Bye, Lark." Tears jutted down her cheeks, and she slammed the door.

The car came to life with a roar.

She backed up and sped off, taking whatever hope he could've possibly had. When she was out of sight, he ripped off his mask and threw it to the ground. Anger seared his insides. He hated himself for being weak, for relying on a crutch he'd used to make living easier after losing his voice, for wanting to hide in front of the woman he loved, who he wanted to spend every moment with. By not taking off that stupid fucking mask when she was in front of him, he'd lost her. He'd lost his angel.

12

Coffin Nails & Broomsticks

utton stopped on the side of the road when the park disappeared behind a stretch of woods and wept all over the steering wheel. This was not how she had wanted the night to end. She'd thought maybe they would've wound up at her place, or his place, without their costumes, without her makeup, without his mask, completely bare for each other, enjoying every inch of their bodies and giving each other countless orgasms. This. Was. Not. How she'd imagined the night ending, with her tears dripping down the front of the steering wheel.

Hands shaking, she called Trina.

"Hey, I didn't think I'd hear from you tonight. Aren't you supposed to be getting fucked out of your mind?"

"Are you alone?" Sutton sobbed.

"What's wrong?"

"Are you alone? Can I come over?"

"I'm alone. You can come over, but are you okay to drive?"

"Yeah, I'll be there in twenty."

She hung up and fought to control her tears during the drive. The moment she pulled into the parking lot, the tears burst free. By the time she made it to Trina's apartment, her body was shaking.

Trina opened the door. "Oh my gosh, what happened?" She drew Sutton in an embrace that only made Sutton weep harder. "What do you need?" With gentle hands, she ushered Sutton inside. "Wine? Whiskey? My granddad's hooch? Hot cocoa?" She studied Sutton. "Cookie dough ice cream?"

Sutton sniffed. "Ice cream."

"Coming right up."

When she left to fetch the ice cream, Sutton dropped onto the pink poof in front of the couch. She embraced a gray fuzzy pillow. Now that Sutton was in a safe place that she knew, she let the full weight of what she'd done crash onto her. She hadn't expected to end things with Lark, but she had told him the truth. Learning ASL was simple. It wasn't a burden. It was actually fun. She could handle that; she didn't need to hear his voice. But if he couldn't take the mask off, she couldn't stay in a relationship with him. No matter how much sex with a masked man may turn her on, she needed more than that. She *deserved* more than that.

Trina returned with a pint of ice cream and a soup spoon. "Here you go, sweetie."

132

Sutton peeled off the lid to the ice cream and plunged the spoon in.

"First things first." Trina removed Sutton's wig and fluffed her hair from her scalp. Sitting behind her, she ran a brush through Sutton's hair. "Do you want to talk about it?"

Hot tears plunged down Sutton's cheeks. "Not yet."

Trina brushed her hair until it was silky-soft. She didn't say anything when she left and returned with a packet of face wipes. Now kneeling in front of her, Trina swiped away Sutton's makeup and tears. A pile of red and black stained wipes grew taller and taller on the pink poof.

The sisterly love from Trina tightened Sutton's throat. She worked on digging out a lump of cookie dough from the vanilla ice cream. "You know Skull Mask's real name is Cal, right?"

Trina's gaze met hers. "You can't put a man's dick in your mouth more than once and not know his name."

Sutton broke eye contact. She'd managed to free the cookie dough clump. Now she was attempting to slice it in half with the spoon. "Has he taken his mask off for you?"

Trina rubbed at the joker smile at the corner of Sutton's mouth. "Of course. It's hard to fuck and keep a mask on. It gets a little stifling under there. Why are you asking? Surely, Lark has—"

Sutton met her eye.

Trina stilled. "Oh." She resumed cleaning away Sutton's makeup. "Wow. So, even after all this time?"

"It's like a crutch or security blanket or something.

He…he's not ready or able to show all of himself to me, so I…I ended things."

"Shit." Trina set down the dirty makeup wipe. "You've been happier than I've seen you in such a long time. Radiant. I'm sorry it's not working out. I thought…I thought he might've been the one."

"Me too." She set the ice cream down and covered her face.

Trina gathered her into a hug. "I'm so sorry. Lark's need to wear the mask may be something that no one but him could truly understand. It's a psychological thing."

Sutton nodded. Even understanding that, it still made this hard. "Can I…can I stay here tonight?"

"I'm definitely not letting you drive home like this. You'll take a hot bath, I can give you a sleeping pill if you want it, you'll have a nice breakfast, and only when you feel better will you go home. Okay?"

Fresh tears filled Sutton's eyes. "Okay."

Trina ran a bath for Sutton and found her a clean set of pajamas.

In the bathtub, Sutton cupped water with her hands and splashed it over her face. The warmth was soothing. Washing away her tears felt good, but that didn't stop more tears from forming. She wished that she didn't feel this way. They'd barely had a relationship. If anything, they had been heading toward having one. All they'd really had was a few moments together in which they'd sought what the two of them could give each other—pleasure and a sense of being desired, accepted, understood. And that was what meant so much and made this so hard. They could've been something great if he could've found a way to let her in and be one-hundred percent of himself. But he couldn't do that, and she didn't want to force him to do something he wasn't ready to do, but maybe he'd able to do it for someone else. She prayed he would. She prayed that person would be good to him and understand how precious that gift would be.

In the bath, every time more tears came, she washed them away until no more tears were left. Then she climbed out and dressed in the borrowed pajamas. Hugging herself, she shuffled out to find Trina holding a highball glass.

"Here, have a sip of whiskey, and then we'll go to sleep."

Obliging, she knocked back the entire two fingers.

"Alright, that'll help." Trina wrapped an arm around Sutton and guided her into the bedroom. "Time to sleep."

Sutton crawled into the bed with Trina and hugged a pillow to her head.

She'd been wrong. Tears still remained.

In the morning, her eyes felt hollow. Dark circles, red-streaked eyes, and a puffy face stared back from the mirror. Even though she didn't want to, she ate a pancake, tearing it to pieces and dipping it into syrup. While she mechanically chewed and swallowed, her phone lit up with a notification. Her gaze drifted over to it. She didn't want to face reality. She didn't want to do anything. Not a damn thing. But she slid her phone closer to read the notification.

Her brows lowered. The notification was an email from a reporter with the state paper and the subject line indicate they wanted to do an article.

Frowning, she opened the email to find a request to interview her, Trina, and their employees about Haunted House of Raunch as a featured piece. Apparently, their haunted house had blown up, socially speaking. More people had been coming, and their social media accounts were tagged daily in photos and videos. David, the reporter, wanted to showcase Haunted House of Raunch as an event to go to this season.

This sort of news would've thrilled Sutton. Before last night. She pushed her phone to Trina, who was scarfing down a short stack of pancakes, and tapped the screen with her nail to indicate Trina should take a look.

Mouth full, Trina bent over the phone. "Oh my God!" She dropped her fork. "Holy shit. This is awesome. Are you going to say yes? You're going to say yes, right?"

Everyone had worked so hard on the haunted house and put all of themselves into it every night. She couldn't deny any of them this accomplishment.

"I'm going to say yes."

"That is awesome. Just wait until everyone else hears about this."

They were thrilled. While they dressed and made their makeup pristine, they gushed with excitement. Their excitement couldn't be contained once the reporter arrived. Fortunately, the reporter was a Halloween lover who obviously hadn't been forced to write this piece. Rather, the reporter had a blast walking through the haunted house and talking to each of them.

Sutton was last. Her friends called her "the cherry on top." Usually the cherry was enjoyed first, but they were saving her as the final bite to end the reporter's experience.

The reporter beamed. "Do you mind if I record this?"

"Not at all. I'm Sutton."

"David. I hear you're the brains of this operation."

Sutton smiled. "Part of the brains. I can't take full credit."

"Your crew would beg to differ. They were singing your praises." He scrolled back through the notes on his phone. "'Sutton breathes, eats, and drinks Halloween.'"

Deciding to play her part, Sutton laughed her character's slightly deranged and flirtatious giggle. "I eat and drink all sorts of things. Not all of it is Halloween. Not all of it is PG-13."

David's face flushed. "'Sutton is a genius. She recognized that people love to be scared, and that there's something sexy about being scared.'"

Sutton nodded. "Fear is exciting. We're complex people. We can't help but be turned on by things that society tells us we shouldn't be. But it's that restriction, that hand slapping that intrigues us. When we're told we shouldn't want something, it makes us want it. When we're told we shouldn't be attracted to masked men or monsters, we find those masked men and monsters sexy. When we're told we shouldn't want the psycho girl with scars"—she pointed at herself—"we end up wanting that psycho girl with scars. Even if it's just for one night of fun." She shrugged. "So, that's what we do here. We give people permission to be scared and excited, on an all-new level."

David typed a quick note. "Is that what inspired you to create Haunted House of Raunch?"

"Yes and no. I grew up in a year-round Halloween shop and would volunteer in haunted houses through my high school and college years. When I became a little Halloween-y in my day-to-day life"—she indicated her scar—"I sought a way to feel..." She thought it over. "Normal. And the only way to do that was to lean in. Far in. I cosplayed for a while as a female joker. My character became big on all the socials, but acting for likes and to give autographs wasn't my thing. So, I considered what I could do to be this version of myself and share it with people in a way that is acceptable, and where they can be up close and personal with a side of me that I don't get to let out in broad daylight. That's what Haunted House of Raunch allows me to do. That's what it allows the scare actors—or tease actors as Trina calls us—to do, as well as the people who visit the haunted house. We can be that part of ourselves that we're told we have to hide away."

"It's a sense of freedom," the reporter said.

"It is. A freedom that is very much necessary."

While she posed for pictures in her joker's play room, she replayed the words she'd said to the reporter and thought about Lark. She didn't believe the mask drew out a side of him that he couldn't let others see. Because he was doing the opposite. He was letting strangers at gas stations and coffee shops see him, but he was hiding himself from someone who wanted to know his edges, his darkness, his everything. Letting someone in could be terrifying. She realized that. She'd struggled to let people in, too. But with Lark, the struggle was more than letting someone past his walls. It was allowing someone to just see him as he was to the rest of the world. She didn't think Lark would be scared to let her in after she started to learn ASL and told him that she didn't care if he couldn't talk. She never believed he'd continue to hide his face after he'd gone down on her, taken her on all fours, and was inside her with a group of people feet away. She never...

"Perfect. The photographer's voice startled her. "Now we'd like a shot with you and the rest of the crew in front of the haunted house."

So she posed.

And posed.

And posed.

The article came out in the Sunday newspaper.

The next day, a local news station called. They wanted to do a piece for the late-night news. She would've declined, but that wouldn't be fair to the others who made the haunted house a success. The news van was in front of the haunted house when she arrived. She pasted on a smile when the journalist approached her.

"Hi, I'm Yazmin."

"Sutton."

"Thank you for having us."

"Of course. Did you want to interview me like this for the camera or in costume?"

"Both would be a wonderful contrast. We can start the interview like this, shoot the haunted house show for clips, and then end with a final question or two of you in costume."

"You've got it."

At a picnic table set to the side of the building, where scare actors smoked when they could, she sat across from Yazmin and did her best to ignore the cameraman.

"You grew up in the Halloween store your parents owned, is that right?" Yazmin asked.

"I did. It was a unique experience that not many people can claim to have. When most kids were terrified of monster masks, I would try them on for fun and go around the shop scaring shoppers. When I was sixteen, it officially became my first job, working the cash register, stocking the shelves, and helping my mom choose popular costumes to have on sale."

"Where did their love for Halloween come from?"

"They inherited it from my grandparents, who got it from theirs. As far as I know,

Halloween is in my blood."

"How'd your parents meet?"

Sutton smiled. "Well, now, they have a classic high-school-sweetheart, girl-next-door love story. They lived across the street from each other and attended the same school since kindergarten. Every year, their families trick-or-treated together. Halloween was a part of their love story. They bonded over it, and they used Halloween and all things spooky to grow closer. Their wedding was on Halloween, and their first venture as a married couple was to open a Halloween store. Then they had me, and passed the Halloween-loving gene down."

"Do you hope to have a Halloween love story like theirs?"

This was an angle Sutton wasn't expecting. She gazed off, thinking of Lark. "No. Their love story was sweet. Mine will be naughty in all the right ways. They were high school sweethearts and neighbors, whereas my love story will probably be with a scare actor who gets my need to be seen. I think..." She sighed and faced Yazmin. "No matter what we may believe about ourselves...we all just want to be seen and find someone who will see us. Like this"—she waved a hand in front of herself—"or in whatever costume...or mask...we may choose to wear."

Yazmin indicated at the cameraman to cut. "That is the perfect segue to continue the interview once you're in costume."

Sutton dressed and did her makeup.

The camera crew walked through the haunted house, filming each attraction for a series of clips to pair with her interview. When they were done, Sutton continued the interview in Nyxie's personal space, seated on the chair where she'd ridden Lark to exquisite orgasm.

"How did you come up with your alter ego?"

"Nyxie is an accentuation of myself. Not an exaggeration. I have a scar from the removal of thyroid tumors. When you have a scar like that, people start to look at you like you're a joker, so why not be one for fun? Nyxie helped me to accept my scars, and she helped others to see and accept them, too."

Yazmin smiled. "That's beautiful. Thank you. This segment will go live tomorrow evening."

Sutton nodded. "It was a pleasure."

As soon as the camera crew left, her shoulders lowered.

Nyxie accentuated who she was on the outside to make her scars more palatable. But what did Lark's mask accentuate? An erotic hunger? She supposed that'd make sense considering how they'd fucked each other. Unfortunately, she didn't know Lark well enough to know the answer to that question.

Just when she thought the media attention would stop, a popular podcaster messaged Sutton through social media. Nadia's podcast, *Coffin Nails & Broomsticks* was one of Sutton's favorites. She discussed true crime, ghost stories, horror movies, haunted locales, and Halloween festivities.

"You have to do it," Trina said. "This is our Mount Everest."

So…Sutton did it.

Sitting on her couch, she answered Nadia's call. They chatted for a few minutes before Nadia began the podcast and their conversation became recorded to share to the tens of thousands of listeners who loved *Coffin Nails & Broomsticks*.

"This year, your haunted house gained speed and was on a different level than the past few years since it opened. What do you think encouraged that?"

"My goal has always been to take what romance readers love in paranormal and dark romances and put it in a place where they can witness it up close and personal. No judgments. Haunted House of Raunch is a way to experience that in the real world, safely. I think we dialed into that in the right way this year and managed to get the book girlies' attentions."

"Did anything new inspire you this year?"

Sutton thought of her first night at the park. "All Horrors' Eve is a local Halloween theme Park. The scare actors there are brilliant, and my experience…" She paused. Dead air on the radio wasn't a good thing, though, so she cleared her throat. "My experience was special. They have their scare actors walking around calling guests *baby girl*. It's perfect. The park and our haunted house have some of the same goals."

"You're not worried that mentioning the theme park will take away some of your business?"

"Absolutely not. In fact, I think if someone really wants to have a memorable night alone, on a date, or with a group of friends that they should come to us first at Haunted House of Raunch for some foreplay, and then head on over to All Horrors' Eve for the grand finale. They won't be disappointed."

"You know what? If you and the theme park worked together, that'd be pretty epic. Two-for-one tickets for a single night. Their haunted house and your haunted house could partner up, swap scare actors, and do continuation attractions from one house to the next."

It was actually a brilliant idea.

"I'd be down, but they have to make the first move."

And Lark's boss did. He called her the following day for a private meeting.

13

Kitchen Sink Cookie

One week before Halloween, with his mask secured, Lark was heading toward Mitch's trailer when the door opened and Sutton came out. The sight of her froze Lark in his tracks.

Mitch stepped out after her.

They shook hands.

Then she was looking in Lark's direction.

Her body visibly stiffened.

He held his breath.

She said something to Mitch. In the next moment, she was walking away. And she didn't look back.

Lark zeroed in on Mitch. While marching toward him, he signed with fast hands. "What the hell was that?"

Mitch held up his hands. "Easy. We had a business

meeting. All Horrors' Eve and Haunted House of Raunch are in a partnership now. Our park is open year-round, and she's going to keep her haunted house year-round. She's got great ideas to attract romance readers throughout. A new featured romance author a month, with haunted house attractions to depict scenes and scare actors designed to look like the book's characters. Author readings and signings before the haunted house opens. Even full-fledged book events hosted right here. She's going to make us a fortune." He clapped a hand on Lark's shoulder. "And this, my friend, is your chance to win her back. Whatever means necessary. She's a woman that you keep, not one that you lose for stupid reasons. You're welcome."

With that, Mitch left.

Working with her, seeing her every day, every night, would be a dream.

If only she'd look at him.

But how could she if he didn't take off his fucking mask?

Thoughts of her and how to repair the damage he had caused dominated his mind day in and day out. He talked to Lori about it during speech therapy, but Sutton's interviews had already revealed the truth.

Her costume gave her power and strengthened her identity, but his mask did the opposite. His mask was a shield meant to protect him. No one could see him beyond the mask. No one could get in. All the things Sutton found so freeing in her costume, he found terrifying—showing the world who he really was in an amplified way? No. He didn't want that.

In all honesty, he was scared shitless of letting

someone in again. When he'd gotten the courage to do that before, when he'd fallen and showed someone, who he had thought cared about every facet of himself—voiceless, PTSD-riddled, a severe introvert with a need to scare and stalk people at a theme park, and a kinky son-of-a-bitch who enjoyed fucking women stupid. He revealed all of that, and he had been too much. The rejection hurt. To repair his broken heart, he'd chosen to keep everyone at bay. It was safer that way, but then he'd hurt Sutton, something he had never intended to do.

He knew exactly what he needed to do to fix it, but it took him a week to finally take the first step and go to Books & Brews.

"You fucking idiot," Benny signed. "Sutton was right in front of you. And you didn't say a damn thing. What is wrong with you?"

Good question. He lifted his hands in surrender as he approached the counter. "I am an idiot," he signed. "That's what's wrong with me."

Benny hustled around the counter, grabbed his arm, and yanked him to the side. "She's been in here and looks fucking miserable. What the hell happened?"

"I screwed up. I couldn't take off my mask."

Benny shook her head. "Have you talked to someone?"

"Yes." He peered around the coffee shop. "I was hoping she'd be here. I didn't know if I would have had the courage to do what I need to do, but…" He sighed. "I was hoping she'd be here."

"You missed her. I'm sorry."

He nodded. "It's okay. I'll try again."

Day after day, he tried again. She either never showed or he'd already missed her. On the fourth day of no luck, Benny took pity on him and exchanged numbers so she could text him when Sutton came for her next treat. He suspected that she also, not so secretly, was rooting for them to get together, and the only way they could do that was if they were in the same place at the same time. He'd heard from security that she'd been to the park to meet with Mitch for more business discussions, but she managed to dodge him each time.

On the fifth day, Amy showed up at his door with a frown, a large Kitchen Sink cookie, and a to-go cup of tea from Books & Brews. "Benny sent me."

"How do you know my favorite barista?"

"Please." She handed him the cookie and tea. "She's my favorite barista, too. I've mentioned you in passing, and we figured out that she makes you tea most mornings, especially when your vocal cords hurt."

"My vocal cords are fine today, so why did she send you?" Still, he took a sip of the tea because it was too good not to drink.

"She told me that you're heartbroken and trying to win the girl back. Apparently, she goes to Books & Brews. She's the joker, right? Sutton? The one in the ad you showed me? The one getting a bunch of publicity?"

"That's her."

"So, you never took off your mask, did you?"

"No."

"Are you going to now?"

He looked away.

"Lark."

He tossed the cookie onto the table. It broke into pieces. "If you came to lecture me, please don't. I've beaten myself up enough for the both of us."

"I don't want to beat you up, Lark. I came to help. Is there something I can do? I can bring Benny a note for Sutton. And then Benny can give it to Sutton when she comes in next. It'll be like we're all in high school again. It'll be fun."

He couldn't help but crack a smile. "I appreciate the offer, but no. I have to do this myself."

Amy nodded. "I get it. While I'm here, let me tell you how proud I am of you for resuming your speech therapy."

He turned away, hating being told that anyone was proud of him, but Amy caught his arm.

"I *am* proud of you, Lark. Not because I think you need your voice or to be cured of anything, because you don't, but because you made the decision to go and haven't given up on yourself. *That's* why I'm proud. But that's not all." She didn't release his arm. "You're chasing after love, Lark. I've watched you become so broken and shell yourself off from the world, but you're chasing after love, and I hope you catch it. I hope you see Sutton again and can make things right."

"I hope I can make things, right, too."

"You will. I believe in you, Lark."

And, damn it, now tears blurred his vision again. "Thank you."

"Anytime, big brother."

Amy hung out with him, watching *Halloween 4* and *5*, which were Amy's favorite Michael movies. He suspected she stayed so he wouldn't be alone, and he appreciated it. Even when she ate his cookie.

On the sixth day, there still wasn't a text from Benny.

Like an obsessed, lovesick fool, he watched Sutton's interview on the news over and over again and listened to the podcast until he memorized every word said.

Finally, Halloween came, the busiest day for the scare industry. He didn't think Sutton would have time for a treat today, but the text came like a beautiful Halloween miracle.

> **Benny:** Sutton is here! Hurry!!!

He dropped his cup, spilling coffee and shattering ceramic across his tile. In a few strides, he was out the door. Breaking the speed limit laws and cutting off cars like one of those jerks on the road, he made it to the coffee shop in record time. He restrained himself a step from the door. If he were to burst in there, the patrons enjoying a quiet morning would think he was there to hold the place up or something.

When he stepped inside, Benny frantically pointed.

Lark pivoted.

Back to the counter, Sutton sat at a window.

He inhaled slowly. Exhaled long.

At the counter, he pulled out his cell phone.

Out of the corner of his eye, he caught Benny tossing her hands in the air.

He lifted a finger, telling her to give him a damn minute. Since Sutton had driven away from the park, he hadn't texted her. He hadn't known what to say, but he knew now. After her interviews, after therapy, after talking to Amy and Benny, he knew what to say.

> **Lark:** I miss you so much, angel. We hadn't known each other long, but in that short time, you changed me. I may never have a real voice. Not one that could hold a conversation. Certainly not one that could yell. But because of you, I am embracing the voice I have. Crappy vocal cords, scratchy whispers and all. You learning to sign was something no one outside of my family ever did for me. That hit me. Right in my chest. ASL is my voice, and being able to share that with you...my true voice...meant something that I can't describe.

Watching her, he hit send.

She picked up her phone from the table. The second she saw the screen, her body tensed. He hated that his name could do that.

While she read that text, he compiled his next.

> **Lark:** I read, watched, and listened to your interviews. You're so brave, Sutton. So beautifully brave.

He sent that fast, because the next would be long.

> **Lark:** After my accident, when I lost my voice, my then girlfriend broke up with me because learning ASL was too difficult. She didn't have the time, found it frustrating. She found my disability frustrating. That shattered me. Later, whenever I liked someone, I approached carefully, only for them to yank the rug out from under me when they realized I couldn't speak. Those rejections made me want to hide, so I did. I found a virtual, at-home job creating illustrations, cover art, and ads. When I was hired on at All Horrors' Eve years ago and put my mask on for the first time, something clicked. With that mask on, I could be anyone.

I didn't have a disability. I didn't have to worry about rejection. The thought of removing it made me think I'd be pulling a Nicolas Cage in *Face/Off*. I'd be removing my actual face. But you saw through that mask. You see me. You hear me. You get me. You accept me. I won't ever take that for granted again, baby.

He sent that text off.

From where he stood, he watched her read his words and cover her mouth. Her shoulders bounced gently.

Fuck. He hadn't wanted to make her cry.

He texted his final words.

Lark: I'm ready, angel.

He pulled his mask out of his back pocket. In his hand, it felt familiar, but for the first time, he wasn't putting it on. He paused next to her chair and gently laid the mask on the table in front of her.

14

The Pumpkin Mask

An untouched pumpkin chocolate chip cookie atop a plate.

A dirty chai latte on a napkin with a bit of foam clinging to the cup.

A rubber pumpkin mask lying next to her hands as they gripped her phone.

She stared at the mask as tears expanded in her eyes.

Someone lowered onto the chair across from her. Although his smell was missing the scent of leather and sweat and the night, she recognized his musky cologne.

It was irrational, but now she was scared to look. She eyed the mask, while in her peripheral she could clearly see a man sitting in front of her. Her chest tightened as she hyperventilated. This was the moment she'd dreamed of. With it before her now, she didn't know what to do or how to act. How ridiculous was that? She'd wanted this. She'd wanted this so badly that it'd physically hurt her when she'd been denied seeing Lark's face. He was before her now and she was struggling to raise her gaze for fear that this was a trick. A literal dream.

Her breaths were shallow.

Tears drizzled down her cheeks.

She shifted her gaze fraction by fraction.

Strong, wide hands that she'd held while walking through the theme park, that had roved over her body, grasped her hair, stroked between her legs.

Veined forearms that had held her.

Thick biceps that had supported himself when he was on top of her.

A black T-shirt stretching across an amazing chest that should never be hidden by cotton.

Her gaze rose higher.

A beautiful neck that she'd kissed, a sturdy jaw with dark blond stubble that she'd held, and lips that she'd sucked and that had sucked on her.

She paused right there, because he hadn't ever revealed anything past the bottoms of his cheeks, above the point of his nose. Inhaling a shaky breath, she continued to the brown eyes she'd only seen surrounded by the cutouts in a mask. Now they were framed by tan cheekbones and dark brown eyebrows. She took in his face and every detail. He was gorgeous. Strands of dirty blond hair skimmed across his forehead, and the sides of his head were shaved. Holy shit, he was sexy as hell.

"Lark?"

He dipped his chin. Then with those strong and beautiful hands he signed. "Angel."

"Hi," she whispered.

"Hi." His whisper back was a breath.

"You are insanely gorgeous."

His lips twitched.

While staring, his face crystalized in her memory. "You...I almost ran into you. Right here. Almost spilled your drink all over you. That was you. Wasn't it?"

"Yes."

"Why didn't you stop me then?"

He signed something that she deciphered as him not being ready. The time she'd run into him came rushing back. At the counter, Benny had smacked her forehead and said she was surrounded by idiots. That could only mean one thing.

"Benny knew, didn't she?"

He nodded, and she rotated in her chair to see Benny dancing behind the counter. When Benny caught Sutton looking, she gave them two thumbs-up. A laugh escaped Sutton before she could stop it. She turned back to Lark.

He had a hand to his forehead in apparent embarrassment.

"You're cute."

He lowered his hand.

"Can I...May I kiss you?"

After a tense moment of eye contact, he snatched up his phone and tapped on the screen.

Her phone dinged.

Smiling, she peered down to see his text.

> **Lark:** You never have to ask for permission to kiss me.

Seeing that, she launched to a partial stand, stretched across the table, and smashed her lips to his. He rose, too. His hand cupped the back of her head. Their mouths opened, and their tongues tangled. Right there in public, they shared a kiss that should be given in private, and it weakened her knees. She leaned against the table and flattened a hand to the surface. A clattering sound met her ears, followed by a moan. His moan.

She broke the kiss then. "Jesus," she muttered. "I've missed these lips."

He latched his lips back to hers.

This time, she moaned into the kiss. "Mm. Wait." She inched back again. "We're in a coffee shop."

They peered around.

Everyone was watching. Then they were clapping and whistling.

Now Sutton buried her face in her hands.

Ding.

He'd texted her again.

> **Lark:** Do you want to get out of here?

His question lured a wet heat between her legs.

She met his eye. "Yes."

His fingers were lightning fast on his phone. *Ding*.

> **Lark:** How close is your place?

"Twenty minutes," she said and signed.

He signed back. "Mine is fifteen."

"Your place wins."

He shoved to his feet and drew her to hers.

"Let's go," he mouthed.

Sutton left behind her dirty chai latte, untouched cookie, and a grinning Benny. In one hand, Lark held his mask. In the other, he grasped her hand. She was jittering with nerves the entire way to the parking lot. They'd had each other in several naughty ways, but here she was shivering at the thought of having Lark maskless and being able to strip him naked.

At her car, he ran his hands down her arms. "Are you okay?" he mouthed.

She bit her bottom lip. "We've never…we've never had sex like…normal people. And, God, I want you so badly like this"—she curled her fingers in his shirt—"that I'm actually nervous."

He removed his phone from his pocket to text her.

> **Lark:** Once my mouth is on that pretty pussy, you won't be nervous anymore.

"Holy shit."

He signed. "Follow me."

During the fifteen-minute drive to his apartment, her pussy throbbed like an erotic drum the entire way. Her heart pounded, and her hands were sweating grips on the steering wheel. She pulled up next to his truck, and he was at her door instantly. He crushed his lips to hers. God, if it were nighttime, she'd be bending herself over the car hood and tugging her pants down so he could take her in the parking lot. And she wouldn't care if anyone drove up on them or peeked through their blinds. Just as long as his cock was deep in her pussy and he was pumping away.

"We need to go inside right now," she panted, "or I'm going to start begging you to take me right here."

Gripping her hand, he led her into the building. In the elevator, he pushed her back to the cold wall. His hard body leaned into her. She tugged him closer. His erection dug into her, and it felt so good encased in the roughness of his jeans. She couldn't stop from grinding into that bulge.

The elevator door opened, and Lark was yanking her out of the small space. They rushed down a hall. At a door marked 31, he shoved a key into the lock. The second the lock clicked, he wrenched the door open. They practically stumbled through the doorway. Once inside, he kicked the door behind them. It slammed shut.

A Golden Retriever scurried over to them with a fluffy tail swishing back and forth.

"You must be Stella." Sutton bent down to pet the dog, but Lark snapped his fingers.

The dog responded right away and disappeared.

She frowned. "I could've met Stella."

He removed his phone from his pocket and typed a message: *I'll introduce you to Stella and give you a tour after.*

Then a soft thud sounded and in the next instant, Lark's hand slid beneath her shirt. His vast palm cupped her breast. She arched her back into his touch.

Kissing her, fondling her, he unzipped her jeans and dipped his free hand down the front of her jeans. His fingers slipped under the band of her panties and located her clit. Teasing swirls of his fingertips had her writhing.

She tore her lips free of his. "You promised me your mouth, not your fingers."

With an exhale of breath as close to a groan as he could create, he dragged her jeans down her legs. She stepped out of them. His fingers rubbed her through the cotton crotch. Her hips jutted away from the wall.

"Lark."

Her saying his name was all it required for him to yank off her panties and position her on the armrest of his couch. He dropped to his knees. His hands shoved her legs apart. Then he fit his head between her thighs, and his mouth secured around her pussy. He didn't ease into it but dove right into consuming her. Her entire core clenched instantly.

She grabbed onto the back of his head, twining her fingers through his soft locks. "God, you devour me so good." As soon as the words were out of her mouth, he coaxed a moan out of her. "Oh, Jesus." His tongue delved inside her, and she knocked her head back. "I love it when you do that." He slipped his tongue out and plunged it back in again. "More. Please more."

And he answered her plea by twirling his tongue around and around.

Her thighs clenched.

Heat oozed forth.

He lapped up what her pussy gave him. Every drop. He shifted back with wet lips. Removing a hand from her hips, he signed *so good*, ducked his head back between her thighs, and fused his mouth around her pussy again. When he dragged the edge of his bottom teeth over her clit, a cry ripped out of her throat. That cry wasn't fully finished before he sucked her clit into his mouth.

She gasped.

He alternated sucking and licking. Every once in a while, he surprised her with the gentlest of nibbles that made her jolt and yelp with pleasure.

Suck. Suck. Suck.

Lick.

Suck. Suck. Suck.

Lick. Lick.

Nibble.

Suck. Suck.

Lick. Lick. Lick.

Suck.

Nibble. Nibble. Nibble.

She came so hard on that third nibble that she bent over him, clamping her thighs tightly, and dug her nails into her palms while grasping his hair.

Still, he continued to give her clit soothing licks that drew out her orgasm.

Once it finally stopped, her body fell lax, and she

released him.

He gazed up, panting.

Breathless, clit tingling, she met his eye. "Did I hurt you?"

He shook his head.

"I was holding onto you so tightly. I could've ripped out your hair. Shit, I could've cut off your air supply."

Hopping to his feet, he cupped her face with his hands. "I'm fine," he mouthed.

"Are you sure?"

He turned his head this way and that, plucked his phone from the floor, and tapped out a message in a note. *Whenever I go down on you, you can rip out my hair and squeeze my head with your thighs as tight as you want.*

She molded her hands around his face and stamped her lips to his. He tasted like her—salty and different. They feasted on each other's mouths while tearing at their clothes. Their hands roamed freely, feeling skin they hadn't seen or touched before. Caressing Lark's body was intoxicating. All of his muscles and veins, valleys and plains. He felt so good but probably looked better. Stark naked and pulsating with need, she stumbled back.

Several feet away, she appraised him. Long legs with thick thighs and muscular calves. A beautiful, enlarged cock pointing right at her. Deep lines cut into a hard pelvis. Sculpted abs and pecs. Veins snaking sexy forearms. Biceps that rippled. A handsome face with a clenched jaw and eyes that zeroed in on her like cum-seeking missiles.

"Holy shit. You are the most gorgeous man I've ever seen. I want to fuck you like this and like this with your mask. With every mask. But first, like this."

He came toward her. "Like this," he mouthed.

Hands on her waist, the head of his cock probed between her legs, so she parted her thighs. He shifted one hand off her waist to grip his dick. As they slid their tongues into each other's mouths, he stroked the tip of his cock over her clit. The friction had her rocking her hips. She gasped into his mouth, and he swallowed the noises she made.

His cock felt incredible. Even just the head of his cock teasing her clit. The moment he allowed the full length to slide over her entire pussy, she shook with needs eager to be sated. He kept up that tease, rubbing himself over her, parting her labia with his cock's head, pressing into her opening but not entering her. The longer he let the game go on, the more she became desperate.

A mewling sound she'd never heard left her throat.

He leaned back, but he didn't stop dragging his cock over her. His lips moved slowly so she could read them. "Tell me. How much. You want. My cock."

"I want it. I want it so much. Please."

His hips pistoned.

She tied her arms about his neck and held on. Still, he didn't thrust inside her. Except, he didn't need to. The familiar tingling warmth returned.

"I think I'm going to come." That sparkling heat pooled inside her core. And it was clear what was happening. "I'm going to—" A detonation rippled out. "I'm—" And she wailed with the orgasm that tore through her. She clutched him as heat slithered free and dripped onto him.

He inched back.

Her gaze lowered to his lips, so she could read them say, "I wasn't even inside you."

"You apparently don't have to be."

"I want to be." Such a soft whisper. Nothing more than breath.

"You can be."

With that promise, he lifted her into his arms and carried her down the hall. She'd never been in a man's arms while stark naked and with her cum soaking her inner thighs. There was something so erotically romantic about it.

She shivered.

Lark glanced down. "Okay?" he mouthed.

She nodded.

He walked through a doorway and laid her on a bed that smelled like him. His body covered hers, and his mouth came down. He worked his way down her body, leaving behind a trail of kisses from her temples to her ankles. Then he ventured his way back up. Their lips reunited, and she used that opportunity to switch their positions. Now on top of him, she gazed into his eyes and studied his features. Her heart fluttered with the love she hadn't yet voiced.

"Thank you," she whispered, instead of saying those three little words.

He tilted his head.

She laid a hand to his cheek. "Thank you for coming to the coffee shop today, for sitting at my table, for letting me see your face. Thank you." She wanted him to feel her gratitude, so she grazed her lips back and forth across his forehead, touched her lips tenderly to his eyelids, and planted kisses over every inch of his throat. She finished to find tears glistening in his eyes.

Oh no. She framed his face with her hands. "Lark?"

He closed his eyes.

Tears leaked out from between his dark lashes.

"Did I hurt you?"

He shook his head.

"Did I do something wrong? If you don't want me to kiss your face or throat, I won't do it again. I promise I won't."

His eyelids sprang open. "No," he signed. "I want you to kiss me everywhere."

"Then what did I do wrong?"

"Nothing," he rasped. Then he sat up and tugged her onto his lap.

"Lark." She hooked her legs around him and combed her fingers through his hair. "Please. It's something. I need to know."

His gaze lowered. After a moment she realized he was looking at her scar.

Suddenly self-conscious, she squirmed.

His hands tightened, and she stilled.

His gaze flashed up, and he lifted one of his hands.

She stared at the symbol he showed her, something even people who didn't know ASL tended to understand: *I love you.*

Tears now came to her own eyes. Her body trembled. She never thought she'd find someone who meant as much as Lark meant to her. Nor did she ever dare to believe that she could be that for someone else. But they'd found each other. At a Halloween theme park, they'd found each other. And they were what each other had always needed.

She copied the symbol for *I love you* with her left hand and lined up her knuckles and fingertips to Lark's. Then she reached between them, guided him to her, and pulled herself closer until his cock slipped into her. Joined, chest to chest, eye to eye, she re-enforced the hand signal and whispered, "I love you, too."

Nodding, he mouthed those three words back, and it was enough. It was everything. They moved together in perfect sync. She'd never felt anything like it before. How his cock stroked her in that position stole her breath and had her squirting on him again and again. He made a noise that she knew had to have rattled his vocal cords, so she quickly pressed her fingers to his throat. "I've got you."

When she did that, he pumped his hips higher, faster and tugged her harder, quicker. The pleasure was so great that it momentarily made her vision go dark when she came. As her pussy clenched him, he came, filling her with his cum and his love.

15

Happy Halloween

*L*ying on his side, Lark kissed Sutton's shoulder and trailed kisses along her scar. She laid her palm to his cheek. Feeling her skin against his, where the rubber of his mask had always grazed him roughly, was a sensation that he'd had no idea how much he had needed until he finally got it.

Turning his head, he kissed the scar on the inside of her wrist. Each and every one of her scars were beautiful. He'd kiss them every day upon waking and every night before closing his eyes. Doing that would be a vow he'd keep for himself. And if she ever honored him with becoming his wife, he'd promise her that in his vows.

Shit. He was already thinking about marrying her. He should probably introduce her to Stella first. He whistled.

The sound of Stella's nails scratching over the floor became louder as she scurried from her spot in the walk-in closet she'd claimed as her "she shed."

"What are you doing?" Sutton asked.

Right then, Stella leapt onto the bed and pounced onto Sutton, who squealed. Stella attacked Sutton's face and neck with doggy kisses.

Sutton's laughter echoed as she rolled this way and that, trying to avoid Stella's eager tongue. "Oh my gosh, Lark, we're naked!" She giggled louder.

Grinning, Lark snapped his fingers twice.

Stella hopped off the bed.

Sutton was still laughing when she rolled on top of Lark. "Does that mean she likes me?"

He lifted his hands. "That means she loves you."

"She just met me."

"Dogs know," he mouthed.

"Do you think your sister will like me as much as Stella does?"

He arched a brow. What he needed to say, she wouldn't understand yet in ASL, so he searched for his phone, which was somewhere with their discarded clothes in the living room. He held up a finger, climbed out of bed, and walked off without bothering to cover himself. One by one, he collected their clothing and located his cell phone beneath his shirt. While walking back to his bedroom, he tapped on his phone's screen.

Sutton was sitting up in his bed, with his comforter wrapped around her. She was gorgeous, but the visual needed one improvement. He tugged the comforter away. She gasped and reached for the covering, but he left it at the end of his bed. Now she was on full display and nothing was more stunning. She didn't need to hide her body. If she was cold, he'd warm her.

He sat on the bed. The way she cuddled into him caused a clenching of emotion in the middle of his chest. With her resting against him, he showed her the message he'd typed: *If my sister likes you as much as Stella, I'll bar Amy from ever coming near you. And now I have the visual of my sister licking your face and neck with a dog's tongue, and that's something I never want to see.*

She chuckled. "But seriously, do you think she'll like me?"

He created another message: *Of course. What makes you think she won't?*

She shrugged a shoulder. "Families of past boyfriends…they didn't understand me."

Then they missed out, and I'm glad for it, because now I have you. And I'm not letting you go again.

"Well, you're going to have to let me go."

He tightened his arm around her.

"Lark, I have to go to the haunted house early. It's our biggest night. We're going to shoot a little promo video to post on social media."

After getting her back, all he wanted to do was spend the whole day and night with her, but he understood they had a big night ahead. The theme park would be packed tonight with people looking for a good time. He wouldn't have a moment to rest. Mitch would want them to pull out all the stops—stalk, tease, scare.

He kissed her shoulder and signed. "Okay."

She began dressing. Jeans and bra on, she faced

him. "Will you come visit me at Haunted House of Raunch before you go to All Horrors' Eve?"

"Absolutely."

The smile she gave him warmed his heart. If he could see that smile every day, that would make the day worth it.

He tugged on his jeans while she worked her shirt over her head. Then he wrapped his arms around her and drew her to him until they were flush.

"You can't hold me like this when I need to leave."

He grinned. *Maybe I don't want you to leave, angel.* But he wouldn't sign or type that, because she did need to go, and he wouldn't cage her. Not even with sex. He did kiss her, though. He kissed her so slowly that he had her melting into him even more. When she moaned, he shifted back and retrieved his phone from the bed. He typed out: *I think I should stay here and you should go to my front door on your own, because if I go with you, I'll be blocking my door with the couch and then fucking you on that couch.*

"Jesus, Lark."

He smirked. "Go, angel," he signed. "I'll see you at four."

She nodded. "Four." With a quick kiss, she dashed out of his room. "One day, I just might want you to chase me and bar the door," she called out. "But for now...I'll see you soon."

The door opened and closed.

He exhaled and reminded himself of a couple important facts. *She's not leaving. She's not leaving me. She chose me. She won't do what the others did and turn her back. I'll see her soon, just as she said. But it's up to me. It's up to me.*

Because she was expecting him to meet her.

The hours leading up to four o'clock were excruciatingly long. Three-thirty, he changed into his black cargo pants and vest. Mask in hand, he climbed into his truck. He arrived at Haunted House of Raunch at exactly four o'clock. He pulled up in his truck, parked, and climbed out. In his hand, he still held his mask.

The crew milled around outside in their costumes, hanging out, taking selfies, and recording videos. Sutton stood with her back to him near the front door. She wore her joker costume, and damn, he was lucky he didn't get a hard-on right then.

Trina gazed over Sutton's shoulder and smiled. "Someone's behind you. He's tall, sexy, and maskless."

Sutton spun around. The smile she gave him was even more radiant than ever before, and he knew that smile was because he came…he was there. As promised. Nor was he hiding. He was there as himself. No mask required.

"Hi," she said.

He cradled her chin with his hand, stepped closer until their bodies brushed, and kissed her nice and slow. Her lips were soft and responsive, taking and giving. Her tongue was silky and thirsty, seeking and finding.

The crew cheered.

Laughing, Sutton shifted back.

He curled his hand around the side of her neck and ran the pad of his thumb down the center of her throat. Her laughter vibrated against his thumb. The feel of it wasn't anything like the vibrations he felt from his own vocal cords, and the tickling sensation made the corners of his lips lift.

She twined her arms around his neck. "Thank you for coming."

He tilted his head.

"I know. I don't need to keep thanking you, but I feel like I do. Because...you could've stayed away. And I don't mean just now but...earlier...the coffee shop...you could've stayed away." Her voice lowered. "I'm sorry for it, but *I* planned to stay away."

He traced her jawline with his thumb, tilting her head up as he did. Word by word, he mouthed, "You have nothing to apologize for."

"Still." She leaned her forehead against his.

Cupping the back of her head, he settled his mouth to her ear. "Still *nothing*," he whispered.

She clutched him. "I'm so happy we met one night...one sexy spooky season."

He snorted through his nose. Then he shifted back to sign. "Me, too, angel." He had more to say, though, so he removed his phone from his pocket and wrote out a message: *We will have many sexy spooky seasons together*.

She laughed. "Good. I kinda wish we didn't have to work tonight." She gripped the sides of his vest. "If I text you my address, when the theme park closes, will you come over? Spend the night with me?"

Nothing could stop him from going to her tonight. "Yes."

On his phone, he typed more: *I will come to you day or night, baby. I don't just want this to be a temporary thing. I want this to be a forever thing. You and I. Far beyond spooky season. Every season. Every day.*

"Me too." She laid her lips to his. "Me too. Me too."

He kissed her back, taking her promise into himself.

His phone buzzed with a reminder that he needed to leave now to head to the theme park. He showed her the alarm, and she nodded.

"Have fun tonight." She tugged on his vest. "But not too much fun."

He shook his head. Never would he have the kind of fun he had with her at All Horrors' Eve. Not unless she was there. He'd hunt, stalk, tease, and scare. But never would he cross the line. That line was only for Sutton.

"When you're done having your fun, come find me and we'll have even more fun."

His hands stroked down her back. He couldn't wait.

She shivered against him.

Her reaction made him smirk.

"I have to go," he signed.

She nodded.

Cupping her chin, he mouthed, "Happy Halloween."

"Happy Halloween, Lark."

He turned to leave.

"Wait."

He shifted back.

"Teach me how to sign 'Happy Halloween.'"

Smiling, he rotated his right hand in a circular

motion, brushing his fingers over his chest—Happy. Next, he slid his hands back and forth in front of his face, almost like he was playing peek-a-boo—Halloween.

She copied him, and he loved seeing her beautiful hands signing those two words on the best day of the whole fucking year—Happy Halloween!

Love Fey

HAPPY

HALLOWEEN!

<3

About the Author...

Love Fey is author Chrys Fey's pen name for all the smutty romance stories her muse insists she needs to write. And who is she to go against her muse?

Each story is a spicy love letter to readers looking for book boyfriends and girlfriends of all kinds.

Fey's characters all have a bit of herself in them, whether that's her Arian fire or chronic pain. And every story includes something she loves—nutcrackers, Halloween, references to *Pride & Prejudice* and *Pretty Woman*, witches, gargoyles, and more.

She's a proud cat mama, a nail polish junkie, and will always write and publish romance no matter who may be against it. In fact, if a story idea may get close-minded individuals mad, that story moves to the top of her list.

Website:
LoveFey.com

www.ingramcontent.com/pod-product-compliance
Lightning Source LLC
Chambersburg PA
CBHW020440180626
46812CB00003B/1332